"Stop it!"

Emma's words shook him from his reverie. He'd only been intent on drinking her in, on marveling at her nearness. "Stop what?" he asked huskily.

"Stop looking at me like that." Emma took a deep, ragged breath.

"Like what?"

"Like you want to devour me here and now," she said, "because it's not going to happen. Do you hear me, Joe? It's not going to happen!"

Joe only caught her by the waist and pulled her between his legs. "Then *you* stop looking at *me*, too." His voice dropped a notch as he wove his hands through her hair and tilted her face up. "Stop looking at me as though you want to tell me something, but won't. Stop looking at me like you're mentally taking me to bed. And stop reminding me that we once meant everything to each other."

ABOUT THE AUTHOR

Cathy Gillen Thacker is a full-time novelist who once taught piano to children. Born and raised in Ohio, she attended Miami University. After moving cross-country several times, she settled in Texas with her husband and three children. *Beguiled Again* is Cathy's thirty-second novel.

CATHY GILLEN THACKER

BEGUILED AGAIN

Harlequin Books

TORONTO • NEW YORK • LONDON
AMSTERDAM • PARIS • SYDNEY • HAMBURG
STOCKHOLM • ATHENS • TOKYO • MILAN
MADRID • WARSAW • BUDAPEST • AUCKLAND

This book is dedicated to Faye Gillen,
the real estate pro in our family, and
the best mother a rowdy group of kids
ever could have wished for.

Published April 1993

ISBN 0-373-16483-1

BEGUILED AGAIN

Prologue

"Sorry to have to be the bearer of bad news, Joe," Doris Walker began via the long-distance lines, "but your dad's house—well, I guess it's your house now—was broken into again last night."

Joe O'Reilly tensed, every muscle in his six-foot-two frame rigid with mingled shock and expectation. "How bad was it?" he asked grimly.

Doris's silence was in itself a clue. "Pretty bad. They sprayed graffiti all over the interior walls and left a lot of debris. It might have been a lot worse, had Emma not noticed lights on in the house and called down to the precinct to report a possible break-in."

At the mention of Emma Wilson, Joe's jaw went rigid with resentment. From the time he and his dad had moved to Evanston when he was fourteen until he'd left at the age of eighteen, the beautiful teenage girl in the house next door had captured his attention completely. He'd never loved a woman the way he had loved Emma, before or since. Unfortunately for him, he had found out just how disloyal and unfaithful she could be....

Joe's gut twisted with the memory of the Dear John letter she'd sent him.

Aggravated with himself for even thinking about Emma's betrayal, Joe shelved the painful thoughts and ran a hand through his military-short dark hair. What happened between him and Emma was over long ago. There was no need to dwell on it now.

Emma was thirty now, as he was. An expert at avoiding those he didn't want to see, he'd only seen her once since he was eighteen—at his dad's funeral, and then only from a distance. He hadn't expected her to come, or Skip, either. Yet they had both showed up— separately, of course—looking for all the world as if they wanted to comfort him, to let him know they still cared.

Joe had been touched. And angry. And hurt. And a million other things. So much so that he couldn't bring himself to talk to either of them. And especially, he thought, not to Emma.

It hadn't mattered then that she was still as beautiful as ever with her slender good looks, long honey-blond hair and bright blue eyes. Or that when she had looked at him across the crowded room she had seemed to want to take him by the hand and lead him off to some deserted corner and just talk to him, to let him talk to her. It hadn't mattered at the time that all he had wanted to do was hold her close. And get away from her. And never see her again. And it didn't matter now.

The truth was, when he was thinking straight and not caught up in the memories and dreams of the past, he wanted nothing to do with her. What they had shared had ended the day she'd eloped with his best friend, Skip Mackabee. The fact that Skip and Emma had rather predictably divorced one son and four years later didn't cut them any slack as far as he was concerned. Joe's love and trust in Emma and Skip had been shattered, their friendship over the moment they betrayed him. Even twelve-plus years later, he had no desire to resurrect his friendship with either of them.

His mind going back to the break-in, Joe asked Doris, "Did they catch the vandals?"

"No." Doris sighed, sounding as frustrated as he felt about that. "They were long gone by the time our guys arrived. We suspect it's a group of kids, and that they're well acquainted with police band radios as well as our codes. We're working on catching them, Joe, and we will, but in the meantime, there remains the question of your house. It's just sitting there vacant, and everyone in the neighborhood knows it. I think you might want to consider putting in an alarm system, if you plan to hold on to the property."

What Doris said made sense, but it wasn't in his plans. "Actually, I was thinking of selling it," he explained. "Now that Dad's gone—" Joe's voice caught and it was a moment before he could go on. "Well, it just makes sense to let the property go." *Especially since I can't go home again without running into Emma, who still lives next door with her son.*

"I understand," Doris said, sighing sadly.

"But you wish I wouldn't?" Joe intuited.

Doris laughed softly, the sound of her husky chuckle reminding Joe of all the good times he and

Doris and Emma and Skip and the rest of their group had had as teens.

"You always could read me like a book, Joe O'Reilly," Doris teased. "And you're right, I do wish you'd hang on to it, if only to guarantee I'd get to see you again once in a blue moon. Once you sell that house, buddy, there won't be any reason to come back."

Joe knew that, too. The realization filled him with sadness, although he had known from the time he was just a kid that sometimes there was just no going back. The act of being sorry, of knowing you'd made a mistake, was generally of little or no value. Whatever harm was done, whatever pain or loss was inflicted, was something that had to be lived with. He understood that, even if thoughtless, self-involved people like Skip and Emma didn't. And as kind of an emotional safety net for himself, he had steadfastly avoided both types ever since. Especially Emma's type. No more pretty women with vulnerable eyes and gentle, tremulous smiles for him. Because beneath that charming, delicate exterior was a heart of ice and an enemy sniper's instinct for survival.

"But I understand you gotta do what you gotta do," Doris continued companionably, "and with you being in the Navy, stationed all over the place, there really isn't much reason to hang on to it. Not unless you can afford to be that sentimental, that is."

Joe only wished. Aware he was due over at the Pentagon in half an hour for a briefing on the new laser-guided missile being developed, he said, "Look, I've got a thirty-day leave coming in another couple of months. Think you can secure the place until I can get back to see to it myself?''

"Sure. It's going to require a visit from the lock-smith, though."

"No problem."

"And I'll ask Emma to keep an eye on the place, too. She was a little nervous, you know, having intruders so close to home."

Chapter One

Emma Wilson woke up with a jolt, the sound of footsteps on cement ringing in her ears. She sat up quickly, a glance at the lighted dials on her clock radio telling her it was 4:12 in the morning. Aware she was shaking, and that her hands were cold as ice, she battled her fright and got up to peer out her bedroom window. All she could see were the budding branches of the lilac bush next to her driveway.

Maybe I dreamed it, Emma thought as she pushed the silky blond hair from her eyes, trying hard to reassure herself that she was quite safe. Although it would've been hard to tell that by her actions, she decided wryly. She'd been jumpy ever since the break-in at the O'Reilly house last week, the second in less than a month. And she lived in fear that the vandals—who the police suspected were teenage hoodlums with an affinity for bourbon whiskey—would come back, to her house this time.

There it was again. Soft, stealthy footsteps, echoing against the concrete. Emma clutched her arms against her waist to still their trembling and, needing to know precisely who and what she was up against, dashed soundlessly to her son's empty bedroom. Thank goodness Bobby was at Skip's house tonight, she thought. If there was going to be trouble, she didn't want Bobby to witness it. Holding aside the drapes, she peered out the window and was able to make out a fleeting figure lithely jumping the chain-link fence that separated both backyards and disappearing around the corner at the rear of the O'Reilly house. *That's it*, Emma thought, sure now she wasn't dreaming, *I'm calling the police.*

As she moved quickly toward the phone, she heard the unmistakable sound of glass breaking. *Damn it*, Emma thought, starting to get mad now. As if those pesky kids hadn't done enough damage to the O'Reilly residence. Now they were breaking windows, too. Swiftly, she reached for the phone and punched in 911 to report a break-in in progress. Told it would be five long minutes before the Evanston police could get a squad car out, she decided to take action herself. She was tired of going to sleep every night in fear. If nothing else, she'd at least get descriptions of the hoodlums.

Grabbing a cardigan from her bedroom closet, she slipped it on over her LIFE BEGINS AT THIRTY T-shirt, pulled on a pair of khaki shorts and slid her bare feet into her runners. She snatched a baseball bat from a closet and slipped outside. Moving soundlessly, she stepped off her front porch and into the shadows, heading for the lilac bush next to the drive. There was no sound now from inside or outside the O'Reilly house. Was it possible the intruders had been clued in by the police band radio and left already, just like before? If so, if they'd gotten away scot-free again, she was really going to be furious.

Her heart pounding in her throat, she decided to check it out. She tiptoed from the corner of her house to the corner of the O'Reillys', being careful to stay in the shadows all the while. Again, she heard nothing. Maybe they *were* gone, Emma thought. It would certainly fit the pattern to a T. And it had taken her a good minute to get dressed. Maybe they'd gone off around the other side of the house. And then again, she acknowledged, her throat so dry that it burned, maybe they hadn't.

She edged closer to the chain-link fence and heard, from inside the O'Reilly house, the sound of footsteps crunching over broken glass. The muted sounds of swearing followed, then more footsteps, faster now. Determined to get a good look at the vandals if it killed her, Emma jumped the fence. Her weight landed on the other side with a soft thud. The footsteps inside the house stilled.

Emma stayed where she was, her fear a deafening roar in her ears. Sweat broke out on her forehead, under her arms, between her breasts. *Hurry,* she urged the police. The footsteps started up again, moving farther back into the house. Relaxing slightly—the intruders didn't know she was here, after all—Emma clutched the baseball bat with both hands and edged forward, being careful to keep to the outside of the vastly overgrown shrubs and trees that peppered the O'Reillys' backyard. Tiptoeing past the corner, she saw one of the windows in the utility room had been punched out and then lifted enough to allow entry into the home.

Deciding suddenly she'd seen quite enough, Emma turned to beat a hasty retreat. It was then she saw him, coming round the shadows at her, moving with such swift, deadly calm that she didn't even have time to draw a breath, never mind scream. Acting purely on instinct, she swung the bat, aiming straight at his midsection, and when he ducked that, at his head.

The next thing she knew the bat was flying out of her hands and she was being propelled backward against the brick. His muscular forearm clamped across her shoulders and pinned her against the house, his thighs like iron against hers. In an achingly familiar voice, the intruder demanded, "All right. Who are you and what the hell do you want?"

Emma blinked, aware that even the slightest movement was likely to cause her great pain. Her head tilted back, and resting limply against the brick, she stared up at him. Even in the fading moonlight, she would know that face anywhere.

"Joe?" she whispered, awestruck, thinking both that he wasn't due back for months, according to Doris, and that in the twelve years since they had dated, he hadn't changed. He was still as handsome, still as sure of himself, as ever. Only now he had that well-honed Navy edge and the firmly muscled, thoroughly masculine body of a thirty-year-old soldier. A body that was pressed indomitably up against hers.

"Emma?" he whispered back in the same shaken voice.

Awareness sizzled through her everywhere they touched. Breasts, abdomens, thighs. He was wearing shorts, too, and where his bare legs touched hers, she could feel the friction of the soft downy hair that covered his legs. And higher, the rapidly rising evidence that he wasn't as physically immune to her as she had figured.

As the strength left her knees, Emma was suddenly, dangerously, aware that the physical impact he'd had on her as a teenager hadn't been imagined or magnified by memory at all, as she had tried to convince herself more than once. It was still real, achingly real. But remembering all that had happened between them then, and recalling abruptly why they were there—locked together—now, Emma pulled herself together and whispered urgently, "There's someone breaking into your house."

He removed his arm from her shoulders. His forearms resting on either side of her, he shifted the bulk of his weight, so that instead of imprisoning her, he was protecting her, using his body like a shield. "I know," he said quietly, not the least bit concerned. "It was me. They changed the locks and I don't have a key."

Emma felt herself go even limper, this time with embarrassment. "You," she sputtered. "But Doris said you weren't due back for several months."

"I was able to move up my leave."

Down the block, sirens sounded.

Joe swore again. He looked in the direction of the sound and realized that the sirens were coming straight at them. He dropped his head and moaned, his forehead touching hers in an intimate manner. "Tell me you didn't," he muttered, then straightened, his golden brown eyes boring straight into hers.

Emma smiled and shrugged, not the least bit ashamed to admit, "I did."

"I'M SORRY, JOE. Truly I am," Emma said after they had cleared things up with the police and the squad car had left.

Joe gave her a hard look, and suddenly the past was more than an unpleasant memory. Emma was uncomfortably aware of all that had passed between them. But apparently, she thought, as Joe moved away from her, his shoulders rigid with dislike, he didn't want to think about that, never mind discuss it.

Nor, were she to be completely honest, did she. She had known from the very beginning what a hard, unforgiving man Joe could be. When she had married Skip she hadn't expected him to understand or forgive her. And she still didn't.

His back to her, Joe glanced at the lit windows in houses down the block. "And to think, I was trying *not* to wake the neighbors," Joe remarked.

The implied criticism in his tone stung. Emma stiffened, hating the way Joe had already put her on the defensive. "Well, you could've called," she volleyed back in a cool, steely voice, "let someone know you were coming."

Joe turned. Hands on his hips, legs braced apart, he looked every bit the rugged outdoorsman he was. "I did. I called Doris." His lips clamped together as his gaze moved from the tousled disarray of her hair to the

rounded shape of her breasts beneath the oversize
T-shirt and the bareness of her legs before returning
ever so slowly and deliberately to her face. His golden
brown eyes fastened on hers like lasers. "She wasn't
expecting me in until late afternoon tomorrow because I'd intended to stop at a hotel for the night
somewhere along the way. But I wasn't tired so I finally decided to drive on through."

Emma still wasn't sure a few hours or a few dollars
merited breaking the glass. Or that the events of twelve
years ago merited his treating her like a common
criminal now. If there wasn't a statute of limitations
on personal matters, she thought, there should be.
Certainly, she couldn't see any benefit in holding on
to a grudge. Picking up the threads of the conversation, she asked, "Why didn't you go to a hotel when
you got here, then?"

Joe lifted his broad shoulders carelessly. "I was curious about the house. Anxious to survey the damage. Not that I could tell much, since the electricity's
off."

Oh, Lord, Emma thought, *the house.* As she
thought of the mess awaiting him, Emma's heart went
out to Joe. He stuck his hands in the pockets of his
knee-length shorts and cast a glance over his shoulder, at his house. "Well, I've got a flashlight in my
Jeep," he said matter-of-factly. "I guess I'll check it
out."

"Joe—"

He turned slowly, his hands still in his pockets. She
could tell by the way he looked at her that he still
didn't trust her an inch.

Nevertheless, as his neighbor of many years, as his former friend, she had to say, as gently as possible, "Maybe this isn't the best time for you to see it, after you've been driving all day." He took a step forward and, her eyes on his, she continued in the same low, compassionate tone, "Maybe it would be better for you to go to a hotel for the rest of the night. Or bunk in with friends." *But not with me,* Emma thought. It would be just too uncomfortable to have him sleeping at her place, even on the sofa. It would stir up too many memories. She didn't want to remember what it had been like to be held by him, to be kissed.

His eyes searched hers. Unlike her, he was concerned only about the house. "The damage is that bad?"

She nodded slowly, her heart going out to him. This wasn't something anyone should have to face alone. "I'm afraid so, Joe." She took a trembling breath. "I'm sorry."

His square jaw set. "All the more reason for me to see it now."

Emma had only to look at the expression on his face, which was so rigid and unrelenting that it might have been carved in granite, to know there was no discouraging him. "All right," she said reluctantly, "but I'm going with you."

For a moment she thought Joe would argue, then he shrugged his broad shoulders indifferently, "Suit yourself," he said gruffly.

Joe was silent as he strode toward his house. If he was conscious of her struggling to keep up, he gave no sign. Moments later, they entered the house, this time by the front door. Joe swore when he saw the multi-colored graffiti in the living room, the whiskey bottles scattered across the floor. Emma felt and shared his growing horror and disgust.

In the kitchen, condiments splattered the walls and floor in big ugly splotches. The bathrooms were covered with shaving cream and dried shampoo. "What a mess." Joe swore, taking it all in.

"Doris didn't want to tell you how bad it was over the phone. She figured you'd find out soon enough, anyway."

Joe leaned against the refrigerator and dropped his head forward, looking exhausted, emotionally spent. Emma was aware what a long day it had been for him. It had to be horrible for him, coming home for the first time after his father's funeral and finding this. Yet they had been unable to clean it up for him before he met with his insurance company about the damage. "I'm almost afraid to see what they did to the bedrooms," Joe said, then finished with an oath.

Fortunately, it wasn't too much. The bedrooms were ransacked, but that was all. "I suppose I should be thankful they didn't spray these rooms, too." Joe sighed as he beamed his flashlight over the walls of the room that had once belonged to his father.

Again, Emma's heart went out to him. Not only was he exhausted from driving eighteen hours straight, but he had no electricity and no water, since all the utilities had been turned off for almost a year. "You look like you could use some coffee," Emma said sympathetically as they walked back outside, deciding that despite their difficulties in the past that she could do this much for him. "How about coming over to my place?"

SHE MUST REALLY LIKE to live dangerously, Joe thought, stopping dead in his tracks. Either that or she was a damn fool who thought they could just resume their friendship as if nothing had ever happened. "Thanks, I'll go to a coffee shop," he said tersely.

Her chin tilted up. The flashlight he held loosely in his hand wasn't putting out a lot of light, but it was enough for him to see the change in her face, from sweet hospitality to shock, and then anger. "Why? Afraid to be alone with me? Or just want to punish me some more?"

"Maybe a little bit of both," he said honestly, seeing no reason to pretend.

Her teeth gritted, Emma pivoted on her heel. "Fine," she said, tossing up both hands in surrender. She strode toward her own front porch. "Have it your own way, Joe. Be a stupid jerk, see if I care."

Joe watched her long legs eat up the walk and then the steps. She still had damn fine legs, he thought. And a cute derriere to match. Not that that was any of his concern.

Hell, she thought he was a jerk! He was just trying to save them both some pain and avoid the temptation to say to each other the dozens of things that hadn't been said when she'd jilted him. Or showed up at his father's funeral years later. As far as he was concerned they had already hurt each other enough.

Emma slammed the door behind her.

Inside her house, lights began to switch on, one by one, until the small terracotta brick ranch was lit up like a firecracker on the Fourth of July. Watching, Joe grinned, recalling without wanting to what a temper she'd had.

The next thing he knew she was storming back out of the house, down the steps. She came toward him, her arms swinging purposefully at her sides. Chin up, she met his gaze with a piercing blue glare. "No, it is not okay," she continued, as if their argument had never been interrupted by her abrupt departure. "None of this is okay. I hate it—the tension and the silence and the bitterness. Dammit, Joe, we're all grown up. Or as grown up as we're liable to get. It's time we stopped acting like kids and started being civil to each other—especially now that you're going to be in town for a few days."

"A month, to be exact," he corrected, aware that his temper was still simmering and that something else had started up, too—attraction maybe. But it was an attraction, he reminded himself sternly, he could not afford.

Oblivious to the nature of his thoughts, she glared at him relentlessly. "My point exactly. I don't want a cold war for a month, Joe. I wouldn't think you would, either. It's not a very comfortable way to live, especially side by side."

Joe sighed. She was right, of course. There was no reason for them to continue to act like quarreling brats. So she wasn't the angel he'd thought her. Making her out to be something far sweeter than she was had been *his* mistake. Hers had been marrying Skip.

"Coffee, Joe," Emma continued, her chest rising and lowering with each heated breath she took. "That's all I offered you. I didn't say a word about friendship."

No, Joe thought, *you sure as hell didn't.*

"Although," Emma went on as if he had said the words out loud, "friendship—or at least a working truce—would not be a bad idea." She sighed heavily, tossing the ball back to his court. "It's all up to you."

If she was trying to make him feel guilty, she was succeeding. Joe had always prided himself on his ability to work and get along with all kinds of people with all kinds of values. He had done so in the Navy countless times. There was no reason it should be any different here, in civilian life, he reasoned.

Even so, there were dozens of reasons why he shouldn't go inside with Emma, Joe realized uncomfortably, and those reasons had nothing to do with their breakup years before, and everything to do with how she was now. Although 5:30 a.m. meant morning to him, it was clear from the sleepy look of her blue eyes that it was practically the middle of the night for Emma. Worse, with her sunny blond hair—which was just as long and silky looking as he remembered it—all rumpled, scrubbed fair skin, and her soft bare mouth, she looked as if she had just tumbled out of bed. And it hadn't taken more than two seconds of holding her against him for him to realize that she was braless under that soft cotton T-shirt—and that he still wanted her, almost more than life.

"Coffee would be great," he said abruptly, simultaneously making a decision and moving past her.

Maybe seeing her in more direct light would banish these hopelessly romantic thoughts from his brain, he decided ruthlessly. A few more minutes with her and the wonder of seeing her again, holding her again would wear off, and so would the latent anger.

Her shoulders stiff beneath her cardigan, her expression both wary and a little nervous, Emma struggled to catch up and then lead the way. "It's a little chilly," she said, shivering as she led him into the well-lit warmth of her house.

"Yes." It was. And her nipples were peaking against the cloth. Joe turned his head in the other direction. It was all he could do not to take another longer look at the gentle, inviting curves of her body.

"If you don't mind, I think I'll put on something a little warmer," Emma said as she gestured him into the kitchen. "It'll only take a second."

"Sure," Joe said indifferently. He told himself he wasn't disappointed. In fact, it would be a relief to have her put on a bra, to not have his eyes drawn to her soft, rounded breasts again and again. Because no matter how surreptitiously he had looked, he was sure she had noticed him noticing.

While he waited for her, he looked around and wished he felt a little less grubby himself. After a day of driving cross-country, he needed a shower and a shave. And for the lower half of him, some ice-cold water wouldn't hurt....

"You've done a lot to the place," Joe said when Emma joined him a couple of minutes later. In white jeans and a long-sleeved turquoise pullover that brought out the bright blue of her eyes, she looked infinitely warmer and more comfortable. She still hadn't put on any makeup, but she'd run a brush through her thick shoulder-length golden blond hair. And he couldn't help but note with something akin to relief that she'd put on a bra, too.

"You remember what a mess the place was when Dad left it to me?" she said.

Joe nodded. Emma's father had walked out on her, more or less, when she was eighteen, leaving her the house as well as the monthly mortgage. Although he doubted Emma saw it that way, since she had been the one to push her dad out the door. "You've really fixed this place up," he commented, watching as she spooned coffee into the filter with quick, efficient motions.

Emma concentrated on her task. "Thanks. I did most of the work myself. It's taken me about seven years, but I've finally got the place the way I want it."

There was no missing the emphasis she had put on the *I*. He watched her grudgingly, marveling at how independent she had become. The old Emma had been dependent to a fault.

Once the coffee was brewing, she faced him, hands on her hips. "Can I fix you some eggs or something to go with that coffee?" She gestured impatiently, letting him know with a single look that there was nothing in her invitation but simple neighborliness. "I've got to eat breakfast, anyway, so you might as well join me. Not that I have a whole lot of time to kill, mind you," she said, glancing at the gold watch on her slender wrist. "I've got to be at work at eight."

Joe looked out the window. She was right. It was getting light. Dawn was already streaking across the sky. But there were other considerations, even if he didn't want to think about them. "What about your child?" he asked quietly, trying not to dwell on how difficult it would be for him to deal with her child by another man, a child he had once wished with all his heart had been his. What would Emma and Skip's son think if he woke up and found a strange man in his mother's kitchen?

At the mention of her son, Emma went very still. Not because she didn't want to acknowledge her son, he thought, but because the mention of him reminded them of—Joe's leaving, and her subsequent hasty betrayal. With effort, Joe pushed his emotional reaction aside. He was going to be here for thirty days, living right next door to her. Like it or not, they would see each other almost daily, at least in passing. The past was over, done with. The fact that she'd had a child with another man was of no consequence to either of them now.

"Bobby's at his dad's house tonight." Emma averted her gaze as she bent to get a skillet in the lower cabinets. "Skip and I split custody," she said in a careful, neutral voice as she brought out the eggs and the bacon. "We're flexible in our arrangement, but he generally lives with me early in the week, and with Skip on the weekends, since I tend to work a lot then and Skip doesn't."

So Skip was still a part of at least Bobby's life, Joe thought, unsure how he felt about that. It would have been easier for him to deal with Emma and Bobby if he hadn't had to deal with Skip, too. Determined not to let the situation—or Emma—get to him, he asked, "How does it work out?"

"Good." She met his eyes, her gaze brimming with emotions she wasn't about to share with him. "Skip is a good father," she said simply, looking, Joe thought, as if she had braced herself for his curiosity about that. "He loves Bobby a lot. We both do. And so we make it work. I rearrange my schedule to accommodate Skip when he has to be out of town—he frequently presents seminars and acts as a visiting professor at other universities. And he makes sacrifices, too."

"Such as?" Joe asked.

"He's had several good offers from other universities, but he's turned them down to be near Bobby and me."

And I didn't, Joe thought. He'd chosen his career over Emma and, if forced to, would probably do it again. Which just went to show how far apart in outlook the two of them still were. Maybe she had been right to marry Skip, after all. She certainly seemed to have gotten a devoted partner and helpmate, despite her and Skip's divorce.

Silence fell between them as they both ran out of small talk. Emma worked with quick efficiency and soon the kitchen was filled with the aroma of eggs, frying bacon and freshly brewed coffee. The smell was both homey and intimate. And the sun was rising in the sky. Was this how it would have been for them if Emma had just waited for him, if they had married?

Not that it mattered now, Joe reminded himself gruffly.

Emma handed him a cup of coffee. It was hot and strong, just the way he liked it. The silence between them was awkward, her glance wary. Joe knew, like it or not, it was time he mended some fences, at least to the point that would allow them to be neighborly once again. It was the only responsible way to behave. And if there was one thing Joe prided himself on, it was his ability to rise to any occasion, no matter how taxing, emotionally or physically.

"You're lucky you have a child," he said. Having had enough of idleness, he manned the four-slice toaster for her as she dished out the bacon and eggs. "I wish I had a family of my own."

Her blue eyes expressed mute interest as she poured them both some orange juice. "Why haven't you married?" She brought the salt and pepper to the table and sat down across from him.

He shrugged. He'd been trying to move the conversation to safer ground, but what they were venturing into hardly felt like neutral territory. "I never met anyone." His gaze speared hers. With a tad more honesty than was necessary, he added, "At least not anyone who was interested in being married to a man who was already married to the Navy."

It was her turn to be irked. Joe had an idea what Emma was thinking—that he had chosen the Naval Academy over her, years ago. And he had. But considering how long her ability to be faithful to him had lasted—roughly one week—before she'd married his best friend, maybe that had been for the best. They never would have been happy together, not with Emma resenting his career in the Navy. And knowing that, maybe it was time he laid off. "So what do you do?" he asked, his manner kinder.

Emma spread jam on her toast with more care than necessary. "I'm a real estate agent."

This was a surprise to Joe. The last he had heard, she had been a secretary over at Northwestern University. He was glad for her, though. It showed she had gumption. "How much do you work?"

She smiled, looking momentarily very content. "Full time."

He studied her, taking in her high, sculpted cheekbones and oval face. With her slim, straight nose, flawless fair skin, and wide-set bright blue eyes, Emma was pretty enough to be a model. Tall and slender enough, too. But she had never had any interest in trying to earn money that way. She'd never had any interest, when he had known her, except marrying and having a family of her own. But that hadn't worked out for her, either. And now, maybe because of that, she had changed. Gotten stronger, smarter, more elusive somehow. He studied her thoughtfully, still puzzling over the changes. Changes he liked. "Do you like your work?"

"Yes, very much." Emma lifted her coffee cup to her lips and smiled reflectively. "What about you?" she asked softly. "Do you like the Navy?"

Not bothering to hide his contentment with his work, Joe nodded. "Very much."

In the silence that followed, Joe realized something. He had thought he didn't want to see Emma.

He'd been wrong. He did want to see her; he hadn't realized how much.

Again, Emma was the first to speak. "This feels strange, having breakfast with you in my kitchen."

"To me, too," Joe said. *You don't know how much.*

She ducked her head and idly speared egg with her fork. "I wasn't sure you'd even say hello to me when you came back this time."

Joe knew he deserved that. Although in the past, Emma had tried to make amends to him, he had resisted at every turn. He'd even returned, unopened, the letters of explanation she and Skip had sent him after their marriage. "I wasn't, either."

Joe sighed and looked at her. As long as they were going to be in close proximity again, he might as well lay all his cards on the table. "The truth is, Emma, I didn't know what to do. Seeing you at my father's funeral made me . . . well, it brought back a lot of unhappy feelings." Feelings he would just as soon not deal with, not then, not when he had all he could do to bury his father. Aware she was hurt, he pointed out, "We didn't exactly part on good terms."

At the reminder, Emma's mouth curved wryly. "As I recall, I told you to go to hell." Finished with her breakfast, she got up to take her plate to the sink.

And a whole lot more, Joe thought, getting up to follow suit. "Right, and then you added to the kick in the teeth by marrying my best friend a week later. Some send-off to the Academy that was."

Pink flooded her cheeks as she put the dishes in the dishwasher. Embarrassed both by her lack of response and his own words, Joe turned away. He hadn't realized he still had so much anger. Or maybe he had. Maybe, unconsciously, that was why he had stayed away all these years and avoided her like the plague at his father's funeral.

Not that she hadn't warned him what would happen before he'd left for Annapolis, Joe reminded himself firmly. She'd said she wouldn't wait for him, not for four whole lonely years. He'd ignored her tearful claims, thinking she'd change her mind when she calmed down and had time to think about things, and entered the Naval Academy, anyway. Two weeks later, when Doris had sent him the newspaper announcement of their elopement, he'd found out just how wrong he had been about her, about everything. Apparently she hadn't loved him the way he'd thought, or she never would have married Skip, and certainly not out of spite, the way it seemed she had.

Finished with the dishes, Emma pivoted to face him. Her eyes were stormy and direct, and as much as he wanted to, he couldn't look away. "At the time I thought I was doing the right thing," she said firmly, as if that explained—no, *excused*—everything.

"And now?" he asked, just as contentiously. His pulse was pounding, and to his surprise, he felt the desire to hold her again. To kiss her . . . just to see how it would feel, how she would respond . . . *if* she would respond.

"And now I know I was too young to be married," she said candidly. "Skip and I both were. But I have a son, so . . . I try to be happy for what I have, Joe. And I'd like it if we could put the past behind us." She paused, her eyes locked with his. "Do you think that will be possible, that we could ever be friends again?"

Joe was about to answer when the sound of a car door slamming, and then another, interrupted. Moments later, the back door opened and for the second time that night Joe's world came to a crashing halt as Skip Mackabee and his son, Bobby, walked in.

Chapter Two

There was silence all around. The adults looked at one another tensely, Skip no happier to see Joe than Joe was to see him. Skip blinked and cleared his throat. "Joe?" He took in Joe's unshaven appearance and rumpled clothing, and Emma's flushed face, apparently wondering if there was cause for the two of them to feel guilty or embarrassed. *Touché,* Joe thought with grim satisfaction. *Now you know how I felt. I thought I had Emma in my hip pocket, too.*

"Hi," Joe said shortly, trying to figure out how he was going to handle this. Had Bobby not been there... but he was. Knowing it was expected of him, and deciding it was the least he could do since Emma had just risked her own skin defending his home, Joe walked forward to shake Skip's hand. "Skip," he said with a nod, because "good to see you again" would have been a lie.

"Joe." Skip nodded back at him, his mouth looking a little grim despite his attempt to be cordial.

At five-eleven, Skip was still three inches shorter than Joe. When Joe had first known Skip, he'd been

something of a nerd, but the years he'd spent buddying around with Joe had loosened him up consider-
ably. He'd grown his ash blond hair out a little longer,
ditched the thick glasses for contacts and added some
muscle to his narrow frame. The years since had added
an urbane sophistication that showed in both his *GQ*
clothes and casual stance.

Gathering his wits about him, Skip continued
somewhat awkwardly, "I didn't know you were
back."

And he didn't look happy about it either, Joe
thought with another jolt of satisfaction. Not that
Skip's unhappiness now could in any way make up for
the heartache he'd been through.

"He just got back a couple of hours ago," Emma
interjected smoothly, stepping between the two men as
if it were the most natural thing in the world. She faced
Skip and Bobby, explaining, "It's a long story, but I
thought he was a prowler and I called the police. By
the time we got the misunderstanding straightened out,
it was time for breakfast, so...we just ate. What are
you guys doing here at—" she consulted her watch
"—six-thirteen in the morning?"

"This is your problem, buddy," Skip said, turning
a stern glance to the bookish, bespectacled child next
to him. "You tell her."

Looking much as his dad had when he was
younger—with excessively combed short blond hair
with the perfect side part and single cowlick, thick-
lensed glasses and slightly geeky, buttoned-up appearance—Bobby rolled his eyes. To Emma, he be-

gan to explain, "See, Mom, I have this history report due today—"

"Which he forgot all about—" Skip added, making no effort to hide his exasperation.

"—and it's on the computer over here. Or the half I have done is, anyway, so I'm gonna finish it now before school." Explanation made, Bobby turned to Joe. "Hey, are you Joe O'Reilly, Mr. O'Reilly's son? That big Navy hero, the one who was part of Desert Storm and all that?" Bobby asked, his bright blue eyes gleaming with interest.

Joe nodded, thinking how much Bobby looked like his mom. And how much he acted like Skip had acted as a kid. "One and the same," he confirmed, warming immediately to the bright little kid, despite the fact Bobby was Skip's son and not his own, as he should have been had Emma just had love and patience enough to wait for him.

"Hey, neat! Wait till I tell all my friends at school! Are they gonna love this! How long are you staying? You didn't drop out of the Navy, did you?" Bobby frowned as this last thought occurred to him.

Joe smiled, glad to reassure him. "I'm a lifer, Bobby. I'll be in the Navy for a lot of years yet. I'm just here to sell my dad's house."

Bobby's face fell. He didn't look any happier about that news than Doris had been. About that, only Skip looked relieved. "You got a full thirty-day leave or what?" Bobby continued.

"The full thirty days." Joe folded his arms across his chest and regarded Bobby with amusement. "You seem to know a lot about the military,'' he observed, pleased.

"Are you kidding? Stormin' Norman is my biggest hero. This is *so neat.*"

"Bobby," Emma reminded him with another meaningful glance at her watch. "The report."

"Oh, yeah." Bobby started obediently for his room, then turned around to walk backward, talking all the while. "Maybe I can come over after school sometime, you know, and you can tell me all about what it was like over in Saudi, okay?"

Joe grinned. He'd been prepared not to like Bobby, strictly because of how his birth had come about, but now that he'd met the charming, energetic kid, he found him irresistible. Even more so because he was a bit geeky and could use some toughening up. "Sure, kid. You can come over anytime."

No sooner had Bobby left than Skip turned to Emma, speaking as if Joe weren't even there. "I'm sorry. I thought he had all his homework done. At least that's what he told me last night. Then about twenty minutes ago, he remembered."

Her fair brows knitting together in a perplexed fashion, Emma murmured, "It isn't like him to forget his schoolwork, Skip. Did he give you any explanation?"

Skip shrugged, looking as baffled and surprised as Emma. "Nothing."

Aware that he'd overstayed his welcome, and that their mutual show of parental concern was making him distinctly uncomfortable by reminding him of all he strove to forget, Joe cleared his throat. "Well, better be on my way."

Emma looked at Joe, as if wishing things were different, and then with equal discomfort and pleading at Skip.

As if on cue, Skip said, "You don't have to rush off on my account. We're done talking about Bobby." He gestured ineffectually, looking suddenly as if he, too, wanted to make amends to Joe, to put the past behind them. "I know it's been a while since you've been home..."

Joe didn't think he could stand to be urged to stay, not by the former best friend who'd stolen his girl from him the moment his back was turned and, with that one foolhardy act, ruined all their futures. "I really need some sleep," Joe cut Skip off curtly, deciding enough was enough. "I've been up all night. Emma, thanks for the breakfast. Skip—" Joe found himself choking on the words, but remembering his manners, decided he could be magnanimous and said them anyway. "Nice to see you."

"Nice to see you," Skip echoed, as Joe let himself out of the house and quickly moved across the yards.

Yeah, Joe thought, the weariness of the long day sinking into him like years of battle, like hell it had been.

"NO, THE LOAN hasn't been approved yet," Emma told her client two hours later, "but I've got an appointment with the loan officer over at First Fed at nine, so I'll find out what the problem is then." Emma looked up from her desk to see Skip coming in the door. Bypassing the receptionist, other sales agents and various computer terminals, he headed straight for her desk. She knew what he wanted to talk to her about. Joe. Dread filled her heart.

"Hi," he said as soon as she'd finished on the phone. His amiable tone in no way disguised the grim worry in his eyes. "I know how busy you are and I hate to bother you at work..."

Emma didn't want to have this discussion now, or ever. Putting it off a while longer, she asked crisply, "Everything's okay with Bobby, isn't it?" *Please don't do this to me, Skip. Don't dredge it all up again.*

"Yeah, everything's fine. It's Joe I want to talk to you about," Skip said quietly, his face so white and strained that she knew she couldn't put it off.

"I'd rather not have this conversation in front of Bobby—" Skip cast a telling glance at the other agents in the busy real estate office, adding "—or anyone else."

Her heart sinking, Emma picked up her briefcase and headed for the door. As she walked she fought the interested stares of the other agents and the flush climbing up her neck. She didn't want her life turned into a soap opera again, but if Skip and Joe had their way, it probably would be, anyway. That morning the two men had behaved like two kids about to fight over one toy, their initial animosity so intense that she'd felt she had to step between them to avoid a potential fistfight.

"I'm on my way over to the bank," she said stiffly, wishing Skip would just humor her and pretend everything was fine instead of trying to read her emotional barometer where Joe was concerned. "If you want to come along, fine."

Skip didn't speak again until they were seated in her car. "Emma, I have to know." His gray eyes probed hers. "Now that Joe's back and we're divorced—" His low voice cracked; he had to struggle to go on. "Emma, you're not thinking about telling him, are you?"

At Skip's bluntness, heat flooded Emma's face. She had known the moment Skip walked in the door and saw Joe there at six in the morning, looking unshaven and rumpled, sharing breakfast with her, what he'd thought. Twelve years ago, he wouldn't have been wrong in his assumptions. Joe would have been there because he'd slipped over at some point during the night. He would've been there eating breakfast with her because they'd just made love. But that hadn't been the case this morning, nor was it ever likely to be that way again. She had to remember that. She swallowed hard, fighting the knot of emotion in her throat. "Joe and I are barely talking, Skip. It's been twelve years since we've had any real contact. I barely know the man."

Skip looked unimpressed by her denial. "He's going to be here for a month, Emma. It won't take that long for the two of you to become reacquainted." He paused, his look hard as nails. "I know better than anyone how much you loved him, Emma—"

Yes, she had, Emma thought. Her heart had broken when Joe left. At the memories of that awful time in her life, she felt her eyes tear up. She struggled to retain her composure.

"How you never loved me...not like that. Even though," he added after a moment, in deference to her wounded look, "I know you certainly tried." He exhaled slowly. "We both did."

Guilt clung to Emma's heart, adding to her strain. It hadn't been easy on any of them, perpetuating the lies that would forever protect them all—or so they'd thought in their naïveté, floundering when the lines of fiction and reality blurred. And now Joe was back, creating new, even more complex and unsolvable problems. Her heart going out to Skip for all he had been through because of her, she tried patiently to reassure him that she wouldn't let him down. Not the way he was thinking she might. "Skip, I made a promise to you years ago, and I'm not going to go back on my word. I know it's too late for that."

Skip studied her, trying to accept the comfort she was dishing out. "But you want to," he guessed quietly, looking visibly depressed.

They hadn't always agreed how to handle the complex, treacherous situation they'd found themselves in, but they had always been honest with each other. Emma wouldn't stop now. "Maybe a small part of me does, Skip, if nothing more than to set the record straight." She leaned over and took Skip's icy hands in hers. "But I wouldn't do that to you. I wouldn't do that to all of us."

Assured of her continued loyalty to him and to Bobby, Skip was quiet. Emma guessed from the strained, torn look on his face that he was thinking about the past. "Joe would never forgive us," he prophesied darkly, "if he knew what we'd done."

"I know," Emma whispered sadly, her hands trembling with the fear she felt. He couldn't even forgive them now, and now he only knew a small part of it. If he ever learned everything... With effort, she pushed the disturbing thought away. That wouldn't happen, she promised herself gravely. She wouldn't let it.

"WHAT DO YOU MEAN you're not going to come to the party?" Doris said later the same afternoon, resting one slim uniformed hip on the edge of Emma's desk. She leaned forward conspiratorily, her short cropped hair a gleaming auburn halo around her face. "Emma, you have to. It's for Joe."

Trying hard to concentrate on the new listings that had just come out instead of the interested glances of her colleagues, Emma responded dryly, "I've already welcomed him home, thanks."

"Yeah, I heard. He told me. So..." Doris eyed her shrewdly, her hazel eyes glimmering with mischief. "How was it? Still some sparks there after all this time?"

Emma flushed. Grabbing Doris by the sleeve of her uniform, she tugged her into the coffee room and shut the door, ensuring them some privacy from the other sales agents and ringing phones in the outer office.

"I guess so," Doris teased.

Emma sent her a reproving look, secretly wishing she had Doris's devil-may-care attitude when it came to men. "One more word along those lines and you're out of here."

Doris sobered. "Joe was pretty touchy, too." She paused, mystified. "I'm sorry. I thought, after all this time . . . Emma, it *was* twelve years ago."

Emma felt the tension at the base of her neck begin to build and lifted a hand to massage the knotted muscles. "Yeah, and I ran off with his best friend and he still hasn't forgiven me."

"All the more reason for you to come to my house tonight, see him again and set the wheels of personal justice in motion. Emma, it's time you and Skip and Joe just dealt with this and did whatever you have to do to put your friendship back in order and get on with your lives."

Emma wished it were that simple. But she knew better than anyone how feelings had a way of coming back to haunt you when you least expected, a fact that had hit her with the force of a sledgehammer this morning. After seeing Joe again, she realized not everything had died between them. Certainly not the passion, or the animosity, or the deep lingering distrust. Was she fooling herself to think any of that could ever be put to rest?

Determined to be pragmatic, she sighed. "I thought we could work out all the angst, too, until I saw Skip and Joe together today in the kitchen. Joe's still very angry with Skip. And Skip feels threatened by Joe. I don't want to be in the middle of a triangle again." She didn't want to feel she was betraying both men simultaneously, as she had during the days of her marriage to Skip when she had still loved Joe in her heart of hearts, while trying to be a loving, loyal wife and friend to Skip. Well, she wasn't married to Skip anymore. But they shared a child, and she still owed him a hell of a lot. A hell of a lot, whereas she didn't really owe Joe anything. Her guilt just made her feel as if she did.

Doris shrugged, knowing none of Emma's darkest secrets. "So who's asking you to be in the middle of a triangle?"

Emma leveled an accusing finger at the pretty cop. "You are."

"No," Doris corrected with a sage smile. "I'm just asking you to put the past behind you so we can all be friends again. It won't be as hard as you think, Emma," she encouraged with a soothing pat to the arm. "Trust me on this. You just have to get started. And the party at my house tonight is the perfect opportunity for that."

JOE KNEW it was a mistake to let Doris throw a party for him. His hunch was confirmed by her first words upon his arrival at her haphazardly decorated town house.

"I guess you've heard what a terrific realtor Emma is," she told him over the roar of the stereo—Kenny Loggins was singing "Celebrate Me Home"—and the steady hum of laughter and voices. "No?" Doris passed a tray of smoked salmon around and kept talking. "Well, listen, she's the best. She's been the top salesperson three years running for the Evanston branch of her company."

"Who's been the top salesperson for three years running?" Skip asked, coming up to join them. Drink in hand, he looked cool and preppy, distinguished and successful as hell. And Joe wanted nothing to do with him.

"Emma, of course." Doris turned to Skip with a smile. "I was just telling Joe he ought to list his house with her." She turned, smiling and waving cheerfully as another stream of people flowed in the door, then frowned at the dwindling bar supplies on the card tables set up in one corner of the living room. "Listen, if you guys'll excuse me, I need to check on the ice. We seem to be running a little low."

Joe was left facing Skip, and this time there was none of the shock he had felt that morning as they had faced off in Emma's kitchen, only twelve years of built-up resentment. He could tell Skip felt the same way. He didn't want Joe back in Emma's life any more than Joe had ever wanted Skip in Emma's.

"About listing your house with Emma," Skip said, sipping his gin and tonic and looking out at the other partygoers. He grimaced as the icy liquor went down. "Maybe you should ask someone else to do that for you."

Joe had been thinking the same thing, but it galled him to hear Skip presume to interfere in his and Emma's lives again. "Why the hell not?" he asked gruffly.

"Because it might be awkward," Skip replied in a stony voice, his own proprietary feelings about Emma showing.

Joe made little effort to stifle a bitter smirk. He stared at Skip and was tempted to punch the traitorous jerk in the face. And he just might if he stayed there much longer. "Well, if anyone would know about making things awkward, you would," he retorted curtly and moved away. The stereo was now playing something by Sting. Normally, Joe liked Sting, but not tonight. Not when he was singing, "Every Breath You Take."

"Joe—" Skip followed a pace and a half behind.

Crimini, Joe thought, feeling his shoulders tense up, wouldn't the guy ever give up? "No," he said without turning around.

"We have to talk sometime," Skip continued reasonably, trailing after Joe the same way he had the first time the two had met, when they were fourteen and Joe had first taken Skip under his wing. Those memories were good, satisfying, but the ones that followed were not, and Joe had no desire to resurrect them; they had been painful enough the first time around.

"For Doris's sake," Joe responded in a smooth, falsely cordial tone, "let's *not* make it tonight."

Skip glanced at him smugly, looking suddenly like the sophisticated, confident university professor he was. Like the guy who had ultimately got the girl they both wanted. "It's not going to get any easier. We both know that, Joe."

Like it was easy now, Joe thought with weary resignation. "All right." Joe leaned up against the wall and, still holding his beer in one hand, folded his other arm at his waist. He stared at Skip grimly, knowing that even if he didn't like it, this was the only way to get rid of the two-faced bastard, short of starting an out-and-out brawl. "Say what's on your mind," Joe ordered roughly, "and get it the hell over with."

Skip's eyes glimmered angrily. "There's no need to be such a damn mule about this, Joe. I just wanted to tell you I'm sorry things worked out the way they did. Period."

To his credit, Skip did look properly remorseful. Joe shrugged, feeling something in him soften against his will. He waved his long-necked brown bottle in a negligent circle. "Apparently, we all suffered." His words were terse, cool, but inside a warm pain had started, making him aware how human, how vulnerable, he was when it came to Emma.

The seconds ticked by tensely. Joe could feel the interested glances of other guests. "Can't we let bygones be bygones?" Skip asked, looking like a penitent kid.

Joe wished it were that easy to turn off his feelings. But it wasn't. Especially when he still carried so much pent-up rage and betrayal. Emma, he could almost . . . *almost* understand. She had been vulnerable. She'd been at a tough part of her life, anyway. But Skip Mackabee was another matter entirely. The conniving backstabber hadn't been in the least vulnerable. He'd had two parents who loved him and supported him in whatever he wanted to do, an easy fully paid ride through the college of his choice, again courtesy of his doting parents. Skip might have had to struggle to fit in as a kid, but he had never had to struggle to survive the way both he and Emma had. And yet, knowing all that, Skip had still cut in on Joe, had still taken what could only be considered, from the way things had worked out, cruel advantage of Emma.

"If you'll excuse me," Joe said tightly, deciding the only way to avoid making a scene and ruining Doris's party was to cut out now before he lost his temper completely. "I see someone else I need to say hello to." He moved off without a backward glance.

Emma came up behind Skip. Her blue eyes were direct and sorrowful. "I heard the last of that. I'm sorry."

Skip shrugged and tried to contain his hurt. "So am I. It would've made the next month much more pleasant if Joe had agreed to just bury the hatchet."

Emma looked over at Joe. He was standing in the midst of a crowd of people, all eager to hear about his experiences in the Navy and the Middle East. In close-fitting jeans and a navy blue pullover that showed off his muscled torso to perfection, he looked very handsome. Very male. Very at ease with himself and the people around him. Just looking at him stirred up a wellspring of yearning within her. She still loved him, after all this time. And yet, there were so very many reasons why they could never be together. Paramount among them were Joe's unwillingness, his inability it seemed, to forgive.

"Maybe it's too much to ask," Emma said quietly, knowing better than anyone how much their elopement had hurt Joe—almost as much as his leaving had devastated her.

"Unfortunately," Skip said grimly, resting his hand lightly on her back as he guided them both over to an intimate corner near the stairs, "it's also the only way we'll ever get rid of the guilt we both feel whenever we think of him." Their glances meshed uncomfortably.

Skip paused. "He was my friend, too, Emma," he continued in a low, defiant tone. "I knew him even longer than you did. I'm tired of having Joe think we betrayed him when you and I both know that there were very good reasons for what we did."

The problem was, Emma thought sadly, there was no way they could clear up that misunderstanding without creating an even bigger, even uglier mess. And that, she wouldn't do.

JOE WATCHED Skip touch Emma's back as he guided her over to the little hallway next to the stairs. The gesture was light, casual, yet seeing it, seeing the two of them talking so intimately, was like a knife twisting inside him. He remembered all too well exactly why he hadn't wanted to come home in years past, because he hadn't wanted to run into Emma or Skip or their child, or be reminded of the single most miserable time in his life.

The only reason he was back in Evanston now was because of his house. He had to sell it, and the sooner the better.

He'd known, of course, he would see Emma upon his return, had even braced himself for it. But he hadn't been prepared to see her with Skip again, or realized how connected the two of them still were and perhaps always would be through Bobby, even eight years after their divorce. It made him jealous and envious and he didn't like feeling that way. The best thing to do was steer clear of them both, he thought.

Unfortunately, his efforts weren't successful for long. At the buffet line, Emma fell in behind him and picked up a plate. "I heard Doris has been pushing you to let me list your house," she began casually, sounding no more pleased about that than he was.

Joe added cheddar and Swiss to the sandwich he was building, then paused long enough to look her in the eye. How did she know that? "Did Skip tell you?" he asked gruffly. The thought of those two discussing him made him even more unhappy.

"Someone else," she said carefully, quietly, her lack of enthusiasm making it very clear that none of this was her idea. She bit her lip. "They said she mentioned it three or four times."

"At least," Joe said dryly, thinking how incredibly blue Emma's eyes were. He'd been all over the world, but he'd never seen a woman with eyes as blue as hers.

Emma let out a small sigh of exasperation and relaxed her mouth. "I just wanted you to know it wasn't coming from me."

Now she decides to keep her behavior on the up and up, Joe thought. Only for them it was twelve years too late. "Nice to know you have some scruples," he said, knowing he was taking the hurt and the anger that had been building all evening out on her but unable to prevent it.

Recoiling slightly, she stared at him incredulously. "And it'd be nice if you had one inch of forgiveness in you, Joe O'Reilly." Eyes flashing, her chin high, Emma took her plate and stormed off.

Doris passed. "Nice going, Joe. I think you just might make her cry."

Joe swore.

Goaded into action, he headed off after Emma, finally catching up with her in a corner of the living room. She was about to sit down on the sofa, but he took her arm and guided her out the open French doors, onto the brick-walled patio. The May air was fresh and cool after the crush of heat and bodies inside the house. Joe glanced at a couple necking over at the far edge of the patio then turned back to Emma, knowing this was as private as it was going to get for them, and that she was only going to give him one more second before she bolted again. And he deserved as much. Since he had been back, she had been nothing but decent to him. He was the one who'd been an ass.

He swallowed hard and said flatly, "I'm sorry. I shouldn't have said that."

She stared at him in stony silence. Ducking out from his light grip, she took her plate and sat down on the low brick wall that edged the patio. She picked at her salad with her fork. "You're never going to forgive Skip, are you?" she said, still not looking at him. "Or me, either."

At the hurt in her voice, Joe felt his own hurt return, and then begin to fade as he recalled sharply that Emma hadn't a mean bone in her slender body. She had been foolish and impulsive, but deliberately cruel? No. "You, maybe," he said gruffly, fingering the half-built sandwich he'd made for himself before finally giving up and putting it aside. "Skip, I don't know about."

She watched him take another sip of his beer, which was now warm and flat. Her blue eyes were both candid and intense. "Why not? Why forgive me and not him?"

Inside the town house, the music—Aretha Franklin now—and talk and laughter continued at a deafening level. And at the far end of the patio, the other couple continued to neck. "Because you were vulnerable," Joe said, looking straight at Emma. "When I left that summer, you had no one. Skip had a family. He was nurtured and loved. He took advantage of you. If he hadn't..." *Things would have been very different.* Joe didn't know why, but he was sure of that much.

Emma played with the food on her plate, not looking at him as she replied in a soft, weary, hopeless voice, "Skip didn't take advantage of me."

It made him furious to hear her defending that guy, when she had to know, now that so much time had passed and their marriage had failed, that he was on target in his assessment of the situation. "Yeah, right," he countered sarcastically, wishing she would just drop the act and admit she'd made one hell of a mistake deserting him. A mistake they were all still paying for. "You just married the guy after dating him one week. Makes a lot of sense, Emma. A lot of sense."

Emma looked away from his hard stare. "It was what I wanted," she said crisply and clearly.

He was able to see from the stubborn set of her chin that she was absolutely convinced of that much. He studied her oval face, the soft kissable lips, the soft touchable honey blond hair, and the fiery blue of her eyes. "You wanted to hurt me that bad?"

Emma turned back to him and released a shaky breath, looking for a moment as if she wanted to spill her guts out to him, to tell him everything that had been in her heart. But to Joe's disappointment, her silence only lengthened.

"What can I say?" Emma finally retorted wearily, withdrawing from him once again. She shrugged and shook her head, the look in her eyes distant. "I was eighteen. I was hurt. I was confused. I acted rashly—"

Joe had heard this version of events from Doris countless times. "And Skip, bless his slimy little soul, took advantage of that," he repeated, making no effort to hide the bitterness in his voice.

Emma straightened with obvious affront. "He was eighteen, too, Joe. He was trying to help." Setting her plate aside, she stood abruptly and paced a distance away. Arms folded close to her waist, she pivoted to face him once again. "Dammit, Joe, what do you want from us? A pound of flesh? Skip and I paid for our mistake for four long years. But it's over now." Her words were flat, final. She curled her hands into fists. "We've put the past behind us and managed to remain friends, and I'm not going to let you force us to start hurting again." Whirling quickly, she started for the doors to the house.

Joe stood, too, and put his body between her and the doors. When she seemed inclined to step around him, he placed his hand on her shoulder to make her stop. He saw she was close to tears and was flooded with both guilt and remorse. It was Skip he was really angry with, not her. "Emma, wait. You're right. I'm sorry." She stared at him unforgivingly for several seconds, then moved out from beneath his hand. Desperate not to lose her, he persisted, "Can't we start over again?" *Can't we be friends?*

In the past, that was all it would have taken, a few soft words of apology, but Emma had changed, and he was only now beginning to see how very much. He felt the wall between them go up as she laid out her own conditions for a truce in a cold, clear tone. "Only if you can let the past end—now. I'm warning you, Joe," she said firmly, "I won't have it any other way."

Chapter Three

Joe stayed until the last guest left. In the end, it was just he and Doris and tons of debris. Garbage bag in hand, he went around collecting paper plates and napkins while Doris stacked dirty glasses on a large kitchen tray. An old James Taylor song was playing on the stereo. For the first time that night, he felt himself begin to relax. As he passed Doris, he stopped to give her a hug. "Thanks for the welcome home."

She grinned and hugged him back. "Come home again and I'll give you another one."

Would he come home again? Joe didn't know. Part of him missed knocking around the old neighborhood; he hadn't realized how much until he'd been there again. And yet...

"I saw you didn't get everything straightened out with Skip and Emma, though," Doris continued as she went back to cleaning up.

Joe scanned the patio for trash. Finding none, he closed and locked the French doors. "Some things aren't meant to be straightened out," he said, his back to Doris.

"Oh, and I suppose you were completely blameless in what happened. I remember, Joe," Doris said softly, when he had turned around to face her again. "I remember how Emma cried and begged you to stay here that summer, to go to school here in Chicago on an ROTC scholarship instead of at the academy."

Joe remembered, too. The way her body shook with sobs when he'd held her in his arms, her tears damp on his shirt. And he remembered his own arrogance, how sure he had been that Emma would decide to wait for him the four years it took him to get through the academy. He faced Doris, knowing she wouldn't pull any punches. "You're saying it was my fault?" he asked grimly.

"A big chunk of it, yeah. I'm not saying I blame you. I understand how you feel about the Navy because I feel the same way about being a cop. There's just nothing else I'd rather do, ever, nothing else I can see myself doing. A lot of guys don't understand that. Hell, my own mother doesn't understand it," Doris finished, smiling wryly.

Joe laughed. "She wants you married, I'll bet."

Doris nodded emphatically and rolled her eyes. "Married with a passel of kids. But that's not for me." Doris paused long enough to stack several more glasses on the tray. "But Emma wasn't like that. She wasn't really interested in having a career back then. All she ever wanted to do was get married and have a family of her own. And I guess she got what she wanted. At least she and Skip didn't waste any time in that regard and they never let on Bobby was an accident, so—"

"So you think it was a planned pregnancy." Joe didn't know why, but that made him feel even worse. Was that all he had ever been to Emma, a means to an end? When she found he wouldn't marry her, not then, had she just decided to substitute the next guy in line?

Doris touched his arm gently and continued thoughtfully, "I think she was trying to fill a big void in her life. Sure, I think she did it the wrong way, but she was a kid and what do kids know? It's time to just forget it, Joe."

"And let her list my house?"

Doris dropped her hand and faced him in mock indignation. "How'd you know what I was gonna say?"

"Oh, just a guess. Or maybe because I've heard it about one hundred and fifty times tonight?"

Doris's hazel eyes sparkled with laughter. She picked up her tray and headed for the kitchen. "Just remember," she called over her shoulder in a firm tone. "We *all* make mistakes, Joe."

"*We all make mistakes, Joe.*" Doris's words echoed over and over in his head. She was right. He was wrong. And it was time he did something about it.

EMMA HAD JUST PULLED ON a sleep shirt and climbed into bed when she heard the soft ping against her window. She sat up in bed, frowning. Another ping. Then another, and another.

Curious, she headed to the window and pulled back the drapes. Joe was standing just beneath it, his hand full of juniper berries, a mischievous grin on his face.

She opened her window and, arms folded one on top of the other, leaned against the sill. It was good to see him here again, in the flesh, and looking so happy. She had missed living next door to him, missed his propensity for surprises.

"Hi," he said softly.

"Hi," she replied. This really took her back. How many times had Joe done this when they were growing up?

He searched her face. "Feel like a walk in the moonlight?" he asked, his low husky voice sending shivers of awareness over her skin.

Hours earlier, Emma hadn't been sure she ever wanted to see Joe again. Since, she'd cooled down; apparently so had he. Even better was the fact that he looked as if he wanted to talk, as if he wanted to make up. Nodding, she said, "I'll be right out." She dressed quickly in jeans, tennis shoes and a hooded sweatshirt to ward off the cool May air.

She joined him as he was arcing the last of the hard blue juniper berries into the dark night. "So what's up?" Emma asked, stuffing her hands in the pockets of her sweatshirt. She hadn't told him, but she liked his military haircut. The short thick layers emphasized the strong, ruggedly chiseled bones of his face.

Joe slid a hand beneath her left wrist. Lifting it out of her pocket, he clasped her hand warmly with his. "I've come to apologize," he said, his golden brown eyes looking steadily into hers. Where his callused palm touched hers, heat radiated and moved up her arm, reminding her how safe she had always felt in his strong arms. "I want to start fresh, Emma," he said quietly. Half of his mouth crooked up in a wry, tempting smile. "Like we don't even know each other."

This was the old Joe, the Joe she had known and loved. The last of her tension dissipated and happiness bubbled through her. Emma laughed and started down the block, tugging him along beside her. "Well, if we don't know each other, I'm in trouble," she confessed, disengaging her hand from his and sliding it up to his elbow, "'cause it's two in the morning and I'm out strolling the block with you."

He laughed and linked elbows with her playfully, the way the two had when they were kids. "Then I'm in trouble, too, 'cause I don't know you, either." He sobered abruptly as they paused to cross the street at the end of the block. "But I want to."

So did she. More than he could ever know.

Seeing the street was clear of all traffic, they moved across. As they stepped back up onto the sidewalk, Joe continued casually, "And I thought maybe we'd start with you listing my house."

Emma stopped walking, stunned, then laughed and shook her head in amazement. "Doris really got to you, didn't she?"

Joe sobered, his remorse evident. "Doris makes a lot of sense. She's a good friend, to both of us."

Yes, she was, Emma thought.

They walked awhile in companionable silence, enjoying the moonlight and the cool night breeze. "Funny, isn't it, how easily things can fall into place? I mean, you've been gone so long and yet...your coming home again, it's like...I don't know...like it hasn't been all that long since you've been gone.'' It felt like days or months to her, instead of years.

''I know,'' Joe confessed in a peculiar rusty voice. ''I walk back into my old room and all these memories come rushing out at me.''

Emma knew what he meant. ''Don't you ever miss Evanston?'' she asked curiously.

He shrugged. ''My home is in the Navy now.'' Seeing she didn't really understand, he searched for a way to explain. ''I guess I'm used to change, moving around.''

Joe always had been restless, looking for what, exactly, she didn't know. ''Do you move around a lot still?'' she asked.

Joe nodded. ''Yes. Once every year or two my orders change, more frequently when we're not at peace.''

Emma bit her lower lip. ''I don't know if I could do that.'' She had lived her whole life here in Evanston, in the same house, in the same neighborhood.

''Sure you could,'' Joe said confidently. ''It just takes some adapting. But let's not talk about that,'' he said as their circular path led them straight to her front porch. He paused at the foot of the steps, the porch lamp bathing them both in golden light. ''Let's talk about my house. I don't have a lot of time, so how soon can you get started on it?''

He certainly didn't lack enthusiasm, Emma thought, pleased. It was always so much easier to sell someone's house if he was eager to help. ''Is tomorrow morning soon enough?'' she asked, unable to take her eyes from Joe's.

He nodded, looking as pleased as she felt that she was going to be handling the sale for him. "Ten o'clock?"

She smiled, as anxious to get started as he. "Let's make it nine."

"GIVE ME your honest opinion," Joe said early the next morning after Emma had taken a brief tour of the interior of the home. Like every other house on the suburban street, the terracotta brick ranch-style home had been built during the early sixties and had three bedrooms, a single living room with a fireplace, an eat-in kitchen, and two baths. Joe also had the luxury of a full basement. But unlike many of the homes on the street that had undergone extensive and frequent updating and redecorating, Joe's had not.

Emma took in his earnest expression. "You want me to be brutal?"

"Please."

Emma sighed and hugged her clipboard of notes to her chest. "You could probably sell it as is if you want to price it below current market value and list it as a fixer-upper. You'll save yourself a lot of hassle that way, but you'll lose financially in the long run because the property won't command anywhere near the price it would if you put some elbow grease into it before you put it on the market."

"I'm willing to do whatever I can to make it more salable," Joe said matter-of-factly, putting his hands on his hips. "In fact, I'd planned on it. So where do I start?"

Emma went to her briefcase, which she'd left on the sofa, and pulled out a brochure printed by her company, entitled "Selling Your Home." She handed it to Joe. "Well, first you need to make the house as presentable as possible, inside and out. I'd suggest repainting all the walls, putting in new carpet and tile, updating the wallpaper. What about the furniture?" She looked around at the solidly built pieces and thought, if slipcovered, the sofa and armchairs both had possibilities. "Are you going to keep it?"

"A few things, like my dad's desk."

Emma sat down and started writing on her clipboard. "What about the appliances?"

"They can be sold with the house." Joe sat down, too, in an armchair opposite her, and watched as Emma made notes, his glance straying more than once to her crossed legs.

Resisting the urge to tug the slim skirt of her demure navy suit down another half inch, Emma pretended not to notice the frank sexual interest she saw in his eyes every time he thought her attention was averted. Her tone businesslike, she concluded, "Good. Now, you could go ahead and list it right away, today if you wanted to, but I suggest you do as much work as possible first."

"How come?"

A wave of blond hair fell across her shoulder, into her face. *And that's another thing,* Emma thought, *I should have tied my hair back.* She tucked the offending length behind her ear, and explained, "You get the most traffic the first week a house is on the market. That's the time when all the serious buyers will rush to see it. Other agents, too. If it's not in good shape, they won't talk it up to their clients. Which, of course, makes the property harder to sell."

"I see your point." Joe sighed and stood again. Hands on his hips, he looked around, discouraged. Although he had cleaned up after the vandals as much as possible, the house was still something of a decorating disaster. "The next question is where to start."

"How about the walls?" Emma suggested, thinking once the graffiti was gone, Joe would perk up.

"Well, the painting will be easy enough, but I have no idea what you do to the wallpaper."

Emma smiled. "I can show you how to strip the walls. It's easy. In fact, I could do it right now because I don't have to be at the office until one."

"Hey, that'd be great."

What she was doing for Joe was no more than she would do for any other client, Emma told herself firmly as she trekked back over to her house to get wallpaper tools and to change out of her professional work clothes and back into jeans. It had absolutely nothing to do with her wanting to further cement the newfound peace between them. Although she was still marveling at how good it felt to be friends with Joe again.

"See," she said after she had joined him again minutes later, "all you have to do is spray the hot water over the paper and wait a minute or so until the steam begins to loosen it, then scrape it off."

"You're right, this is easy." Joe peeled off the first long strip. "So how's your dad?"

Emma sprayed water over the next section of paper. She didn't mind the personal question; she was just as eager to get caught up with his life as he was with hers. "Dad's in Vegas at the moment, performing at one of the casinos. He's in this band that plays for the blue-hair-and-champagne set. At least that's how he puts it."

"Blue-hair-and-champagne set?" Joe echoed. Finished removing a long strip of the ugly wallpaper, he let it drop to the floor.

"Senior citizens, Lawrence Welk fans," Emma supplied at Joe's baffled look. "They like music you can fox-trot to and Dad and his band supply it." Proudly, she continued, "They've been everywhere the past thirteen years—cruise ships, hotels, anniversary bashes, society weddings. He has an agent in New York who books the band and they're very successful."

"He's happy?"

Emma nodded, unable to adequately express her profound relief about that. "Oh, yes, more than he ever was when I was a kid."

Joe frowned and dragged a kitchen chair over to the section of wall Emma had just dampened. Stepping back up beside her, he said grimly, "He always made you feel like a chain around his neck, didn't he?"

Emma dragged her chair farther to the left, too. She concentrated on wetting down the next section of wall as she explained, "He didn't mean to, Joe. But when Mama died and he had to come back to take care of me, well, it was hard for him, giving up a life on the road to teach junior-high band students how to play sax.''

"It wasn't that bad for him. He wasn't completely cut off from performing. He had night jobs, in clubs,'' Joe reminded her. Emma knew he was thinking of all the times she'd had to scrape up a dinner, alone, because her dad was either off at a rehearsal or playing a gig. Emma knew that in his own somewhat selfish way her dad had loved her and still did, but Joe was right. Hers hadn't been a very happy childhood. She'd felt like an unwanted burden so much of the time.

Nevertheless, Emma found herself defending her father, maybe because aside from Bobby and Skip, he was the only family she had. "Before I was old enough not to need a sitter there were a lot of years when he didn't have the money to hire someone to watch me, so he didn't work in the clubs at all." Although maybe he should have, Emma thought. Her dad had always been happier playing gigs than he ever was teaching music in school. And when he had been miserable, she had been miserable, too.

As they reached the first corner, Joe stepped back to look at the bare wallboard. Behind him, Emma couldn't help but note how the gray sweat pants he'd put on hugged his lower body like a soft cotton glove, clearly delineating the long sinewy lines of his hips and legs. His Navy T-shirt did the same thing for the powerful lines of his shoulders, arms, and back. No doubt about it, he was solid male muscle from head to toe.

"You don't regret sending him off like that?" Joe asked, dragging her back to the present. While waiting for her to answer, he looked at her carefully.

Again, Emma thought about her dad. For a year or so after she had encouraged her dad to follow his dream, she had sometimes wished that she hadn't been quite so selfless at the tender age of eighteen. But if her dad had stayed she would have always felt guilty for ruining his life and cutting short his dream of a music career on the road. Her dad might never have meant to make her feel she was a noose around his neck, but he had, in so many ways. Emma never wanted to feel that way again.

She dragged her chair to midpoint of the next wall. "Our relationship is better now because it's built on want-to's instead of have-to's."

Joe looked at her in the old way, with protectiveness and respect. "Does he ever visit?" he asked.

"If he happens to be in Chicago, which to tell the truth isn't often. Every once in a while Bobby and I go visit him."

"What does Bobby think?"

Emma paused long enough to refill her sprayer bottle with scalding water. "He and Dad get along but they don't have a whole lot in common. To Dad's disappointment, Bobby's not interested in music at all. He likes computers and gadgets and more intellectual pursuits." She paused. "What about you? Do you miss your dad?"

Joe nodded, his look one of fleeting sadness. "I wish we'd had more time. I wish—"

"What?" Emma asked gently when Joe didn't go on.

Joe scraped at the next strip of wallpaper with more force than was necessary. "I wish that we had been as close as a father and son should've been."

Joe hadn't gotten along with his father very well, either during the four years he and Emma had lived as next-door neighbors. It was one of the things they'd had in common. Both of them were only children being reared by single fathers in houses where friction seemed to be the norm. "The two of you still argued?" She remembered how the fights with his dad had always torn Joe up inside, though he'd never talked much about what was said during them.

Joe nodded, his expression turning both sad and introspective. "It never took long. I mean I loved him and I know he loved me, but he was always making excuses for things, rationalizing his actions and everyone else's. That drove me crazy and he knew it and that drove him crazy. And then we were off, saying all sorts of crazy things to each other. Bringing up things in the past that would have been much better left unsaid."

Emma didn't know about that. She'd always felt a good healthy argument could clear the air. She also felt he was beating himself up unnecessarily. "Don't you think a lot of what we felt back then was the normal teenage angst?" she asked gently. "I mean, some of my women friends at work have teenage daughters and it seems like they're always fighting with them."

Joe was silent.

Emma tried to coax a smile out of him. "Makes me kind of glad that I was a girl, you know? I think if I'd been a son, my father and I would probably have argued as much as you and your dad." Instead of suffering the long moody silences that had made them both just as unhappy.

Joe braced a shoulder against the wall. "You think that's all it was with my dad and me, that we were both male?"

Emma's eyes rested absently on the powerful curve of Joe's biceps, visible beneath the sleeve of the Navy T-shirt, before returning to his golden brown eyes. "What else could it have been?" she asked, frustrated at the sudden way this conversation had become almost one-sided.

Joe went back to scraping and didn't answer. Emma was reminded of the past, of the way he had always walked away from difficult emotional issues rather than discuss them.

"You know, you don't have to stay and help me with this," he said after a moment, his tone pleasant as he turned to face her. "I've got the hang of it."

He didn't *look* as if he wanted her to go, Emma thought. "I don't mind. Really."

A short hour later they had finished. "I told you it would go fast," Emma said, watching as Joe crushed the last of the old wallpaper, put it into a garbage bag and stacked it with the others in a corner of the garage.

He grinned and brushed a hand down her nose, eliciting tingles wherever skin contacted skin. "You've got chalky white dust all over you."

Telling herself the sensual electricity she felt whenever she was with Joe was more remembered and romanticized than real, Emma took a swipe at his cheek and came up with a white fingertip. "So do you. It's wallpaper sizing."

His eyes crinkled at the corners as he smiled. Fighting the wave of attraction that had been building between them all morning, Emma stepped back slightly and said, "I'm going to need you to sign a selling agreement."

"No problem."

He smiled again and this time she smiled with him. "When would be a good time for me to bring it by?"

"When's good for you?"

Looking into his dark-lashed eyes, Emma realized it would be so easy to fall in love with him again. And yet, because he was leaving again, this time for good, she knew that this wasn't something she wanted to do. Out loud, she heard herself saying calmly, "I have to be at the office until six, but I could type it up and be over here by about six-thirty."

Joe shoved an impatient hand through the soft dark layers of his hair. "Fine, but you don't have to come back over here. Just give me a call when you get in and I'll come over there and sign it."

Emma tore her eyes from the softness of his lips. "Fair enough."

Unfortunately for Emma, her day at work did not go as smoothly as her morning with Joe. The phones rang off the hook. A client called to complain about the rudeness of an agent from a competing firm, demanding Emma do something about it, and Skip called, sounding very upset as he demanded without preamble, "Have you checked your mail today?"

Emma stiffened, every cell in her body on red alert. "No," she admitted warily, knowing by the tone of Skip's voice this was something bad. "It hadn't come by the time I left the house."

"Guess what I got? A progress report from Bobby's school. He's flunking *algebra*. Can you believe it?" Skip finished incredulously.

No, Emma couldn't. "I thought he was acing that class," she countered, stunned. In fact, Bobby *always* aced math.

"He was. Up until this past six weeks."

"So what happened?"

"I don't know." Exasperation colored Skip's low tone. "I'll let you talk to him."

"Mom? Listen, don't be mad," Bobby began earnestly. "I couldn't help it. I just . . . I think the work is too hard for me. I think—I think maybe I should repeat eighth grade."

Before Emma had a chance to say anything, Skip was back on the line. "Did you hear that?" he said. "Can you believe it?"

"No, but I'm sure there's a good reason, Skip," Emma said. She always took school problems more calmly than Skip, who was a teacher.

"I have yet to hear it."

"Could we talk about this later?" Emma asked, smiling as the clients she'd been expecting walked through the door. She waved them on over to her desk. "I've got to show a house."

"Sure. I'll come over tonight. Seven, seven-thirty okay with you?"

"Fine," Emma said. Unfortunately, she was later than she expected getting home. Joe, who'd been sitting on the front stoop watching for her, met her as she parked in the drive.

"I've got my pen," he said, holding it up for proof.

Emma smiled and held up her briefcase as she walked rapidly up to greet him, her high heels clicking on the cement walk. "I've got the listing agreement," she replied. If only all her other clients were as easy to work with and as patient as Joe looked now. "Why don't you come on in," she invited. "You can read the listing agreement and I'll answer any questions you might have."

"That'd be great."

She noticed he'd shaved and showered and put on fresh, ironed clothes. After-shave clung to his jaw. Both subtle and brisk, it smelled of sandalwood and spice. "Going out tonight?" she asked in an effort to make casual conversation. He looked—and smelled— as if he had a date. And that bothered her, though she'd be damned if she'd admit to herself why.

Joe nodded. "Some of the guys called. We're going down to shoot some pool."

Emma smiled. "Sounds fun."

Joe grinned back, looking every bit the man's man he was and always had been. "It will be."

Leaving Joe to peruse the contract at his leisure without her standing over his shoulder, she went into the kitchen to fix them both a cold drink. As she expected, Joe had a few questions. She answered them patiently, and then watched as he signed his name at the bottom of the typewritten pages.

Car doors slammed in the driveway. Taking that as a signal to go, Joe stood and handed her the signed pages just as Bobby skulked into the house, Skip close on his heels.

Skip took in the two of them, his displeasure with their son momentarily forgotten. "Joe," he said between clenched teeth, followed with a formal nod.

Emma held her breath, waiting for Joe's reaction.

"Skip. Nice to see you." Joe extended his hand. He slanted a glance at Emma. "Emma's firm is listing my house," he said, by way of explanation for his presence.

Emma was pleased and grateful for Joe's graciousness. He wasn't the type of man who explained himself, but he had—tonight—for her benefit.

"Hiya, Joe!" Oblivious to the unusual tenseness in Skip's frame, or the veiled but questioning looks Skip was giving Emma, Bobby gave Joe a high five. "When are you going to show me all your medals?"

"I didn't bring them with me," Joe admitted gently as Bobby's face fell. Looking as if he were sorry he had disappointed Bobby, he continued easily, "But I'd be glad to show you my Jeep. Want to go have a look-see, that is, if it's okay with your mom and dad?"

Emma nodded her permission, as did Skip—reluctantly. "Emma and I need to talk, anyway," Skip said.

"I know," Bobby moaned morosely, pressing both hands to the sides of his head like a vise. "About me." He trooped out the door after Joe. "We're probably better off not hearing that," Bobby told Joe. Joe laughed, his husky chuckle echoing in the still evening air.

Skip looked back at Emma. Now that Bobby and Joe were gone, the gloves were off. "You're listing his house?" Skip repeated incredulously, his disapproval evident.

Emma fought a flush. She had nothing to feel guilty or ashamed about, and she'd be darned if she would let Skip make her feel otherwise. "Yes. I am," she retorted evenly, holding his gaze.

Skip shook his head in mute remonstration and then looked at her as if she were a nine-year-old, and not a particularly bright one at that. "Why?" he demanded curtly, his usually pleasant personality nowhere in evidence. "Aren't things difficult enough for you, just having Joe next door again?"

They were and they weren't, Emma thought as she squared her shoulders and prepared to face off with her ex-husband. It was tough seeing Joe so much, mainly because every time she looked at him she remembered so much. But that was neither here nor there. Right now the issue was Skip's lack of rights when it came to dictating the terms of her life. "Listing houses is what I do," she said tightly.

"I know that." Aggravation showed in the tense set of Skip's lips. "The question is why, Emma?" He took a step nearer, his close proximity reminding her of all they had once been to one another, too, and in many ways still were. His voice lowered conspiratorially. "Why would you set yourself up like that?"

"Because Joe and I are friends again." And, she thought honestly, *I want to spend time with him. I want to get to know him again.*

Skip absorbed her words, his expression growing more displeased and incredulous with every passing moment. He shook his head at her, looking as if he thought her the worst kind of fool. "Friends," he echoed heavily. "For how long?" When Emma didn't reply, he reminded in a harsh, unremitting tone, "Joe broke your heart once, Emma. He all but destroyed you. Do you really want him to do it again?"

Chapter Four

"Wait a minute, Skip," Emma said, her voice tight with annoyance. "You are *way* out of line."

"Am I?"

Emma's shoulders were rigid with tension as she stood her ground. "I don't have to justify myself to you or anyone else."

"No, you don't," Skip volleyed back angrily, his glance whipping over her from head to toe before returning to her upturned face. "You're an adult. You can do whatever you want. You can hurt me as much as you want, and there's not a damn thing I can do about it."

At the pain quavering in his low voice, Emma held up both hands as if to ward off a physical blow. "Skip, don't," she beseeched, her own voice trembling, too. Hadn't they already hurt each other enough in the past, she thought desperately, and all because of Joe?

"Don't what?" Skip asked, stepping heedlessly nearer, his gray eyes shining jealously. "Don't tell the truth? Don't ask you to accept the consequences of what you're asking—no, begging—to happen?" His voice dropped an intimate notch. "I thought we could be honest with each other, Emma. I thought we could be honest with ourselves."

He was right. He knew things about her—unvarnished truths—that no one else did. How weak she'd been where Joe was concerned, how devastated she'd been when Joe left.

Silence fell as they regarded each other. Guilt flooded Emma. She had never meant to hurt Skip, especially when she knew he was just trying to protect the life they had for themselves with Bobby. Divorced or no, the three of them were still and always would be a family.

Her pulse racing, Emma admitted quietly, "I wish things were different, Skip. I wish I could change the past." And she wished she had never gotten involved with Joe, or made love with him, or known what it was like to sleep wrapped in his arms. But she did know, and like it or not, there was no erasing those memories—or the ones of the heartbreaking time of her life that followed.

To Emma's relief, Skip calmed down. "You were so young, Emma. We all were," he soothed, letting her know that despite his jealousy over Joe, he still understood that much.

Emma turned away, the shame she felt coming back full force. "There's still no excuse for what I did," she said.

"Don't be so hard on yourself, Emma. You did the best you could. Just like I did. Besides," he reasoned on a lengthy sigh, "back then we had no idea how all this would turn out. If we had foreseen the complica-

tions—well, who knows what we would've done."
Hands on her shoulders, he guided her around to face
him, letting her know with a single look that he didn't
blame her for what had happened. "But we're older
now," he continued, his usual scholarly look returning to his handsome face. "We have the wisdom of
experience to guide us. And we have Bobby to think
about."

Emma released the breath she had been holding. "I
would never hurt Bobby."

"Not intentionally, no," Skip dropped his hold on
her and stepped back. "But any blowup with
Joe . . . how would our son feel if he knew?"

Again, Emma was at a loss. This was such an incredibly difficult situation. She knew she owed Skip a
lot, she and Bobby both did. He was the only family
she'd had since her father had left, and she had needed
his support all these years. He'd been a good friend to
her and a loving father to Bobby.

However, she reasoned securely, that still didn't give
him the right to run her life. Only she knew what was
best for herself. And what was best was calling an end
to their long cold war with Joe.

"I am going to list his house. In these economic
times I can't afford to turn down the commission."

Skip's head lifted sharply and he looked at her in a
way that let her know he saw through her excuses.
"It's not just the money goading you into this,
Emma."

He was right, it wasn't. "I want us all to be friends.
My helping Joe do this is a good way to ensure that
will happen."

Skip watched her, unconvinced, maybe even a little disappointed. Nervously, he combed his fingers through his ash blond hair. "I still think it's an unnecessary risk."

Emma had an idea what Skip was thinking, that she'd be in bed with Joe again before week's end. But he was wrong. "You don't trust me to be able to handle myself?" she challenged harshly.

Skip turned away and didn't answer, looking for a moment as if just the idea of Joe and Emma together was too much for him to handle. "I just don't want to see you hurt," he said.

"I won't be," Emma said calmly, although she was less sure of that than she sounded. She knew she could be hurt very easily by Joe, very easily.

Several seconds passed. Neither of them spoke. Finally, Skip seemed to know he wasn't going to be able to change her mind. "At least be careful," he said. Then he reminded her, "He's only going to be here thirty days."

How well Emma knew that. Not that it mattered. She didn't intend to get involved with Joe at all—just resume their friendship on a very cursory, innocent level.

Hoping to drop all talk of Joe, she prompted, "You said you wanted to talk to me about the progress report from Bobby's school. Do you think he needs a tutor?"

Skip shook his head, his attention once again focused on the problems of the son they both loved so very much. "No. I spent most of the afternoon going over the lessons with him." Skip's glance narrowed speculatively and he shook his head in frustration. "He knows the stuff, Emma."

Feeling immediately closer to Skip now that the talk was back to familial ground, Emma asked, "Then why is he failing?"

Skip followed Emma into her kitchen and watched while she fixed them both tall, icy glasses of lemonade. "For one thing, he hasn't been turning in his homework, so he's been getting zeros on his daily grades. And he hasn't been finishing his tests."

"Have you talked to Bobby?" Emma asked as she added a slice of lemon to each glass and handed Skip his.

Skip nodded, then took a lengthy sip of his drink before saying, "He's promised me he'll do better and get his grade up to passing by the end of the six weeks. His teacher said extra credit is possible, so that will help. Still, this will blow his average for the six weeks."

Emma sighed. "It's probably just a stage," she theorized, taking comfort in the fact that all parents had problems of some sort or another with their kids.

"I hope so," Skip said, but he looked nowhere near as convinced of that as Emma hoped he would be.

"EVERYTHING OKAY?" Joe asked Emma as the two of them headed down to his basement to sort through the years of accumulated junk to see if there was enough potential "merchandise" down there to merit having a yard sale. "You seem a little down," he continued as he pulled a cord to turn on an overhead light.

Emma knew he was thinking about the tension he'd seen between her and Skip. Reminded how easily Joe had always been able to see into her soul, and fearing what would happen if he did, she shrugged off his concern. "It's nothing."

Joe nodded and didn't press for further details, but she could tell by the way he promptly averted his glance that he was hurt. In the past when they'd been friends, she hadn't hesitated to confide in him.

Deciding abruptly she had to tell him something, Emma continued, "Bobby is suddenly having trouble with his algebra."

Joe shifted several boxes marked Kitchen. "Can't the two of you help him?"

Emma rescued a birdcage and put it in the pile of salable goods she was stockpiling on her side of the basement. "We can and do tutor him when necessary," Emma admitted, stepping over an embroidered footstool with a torn cover and picking up a magazine rack. Finding it in good shape, too, she carried it back to the pile of goods that could be sold as is. "But that's not the problem," she continued confidentially. "Skip says he knows the material."

"Then what's the problem?" Joe gave her a quizzical look as he started his own pile of salable goods.

"That's just it." Emma released a beleaguered sigh as Joe inspected an ancient tennis racket. "We don't know. I'm hoping it's just a stage. Skip isn't so certain." She frowned, perturbed. "Bobby's always been so conscientious."

Joe's lips had tightened at her mention of Skip, but he relaxed again as he added the racket to the pile of yard sale goods and asked, "What grade is Bobby in?"

Emma smiled, thinking how fast he'd grown up, and how pleased she was, this little glitch included, at the way he'd turned out. "Eighth."

"Eighth," Joe echoed, surprised, and Emma knew what Joe was thinking. Bobby was awfully small to be in eighth grade. Young, too, at just eleven.

"He skipped two grades," she informed Joe matter-of-factly, watching as he dug into the kitchen boxes and found an assortment of mismatched dishes. "Second and fifth. Even in the accelerated classes, he wasn't being challenged intellectually, so at the advice of his teachers we moved him on."

Emma looked over at Joe, saw a smudge of dirt on his cheek and resisted the urge to cover the distance between them and remove it. "Did skipping the grades help?" he asked, frowning as he threw a chipped dish into the trash.

Emma felt her mood brighten at his continued interest in her son. But she felt that way when anyone expressed an interest in Bobby, she reminded herself. "Oh, yes. In fact, it's gone very well."

"Until now," Joe qualified with a nonjudgmental glance.

She nodded, relieved he understood.

Finished with the first box, Joe started on the second. "Maybe he has his mind on a girl," he theorized absently, as he paused to examine a skillet with a broken handle. "I know firsthand how distracting that can be. Gosh, didn't Dad ever throw anything away?" he finished with a perplexed shake of his head.

"It doesn't look that way, does it?" Emma murmured sympathetically as she knelt next to a box of books and began to sort through them. Shakespeare's plays... Isaac Asimov... a Home-Fix-It manual... Meals in Minutes... But it was impossible for her to concentrate on the task at hand. Joe's theory about Bobby's academic inattentiveness, so innocently spoken, had alerted her to the possibility that Bobby's current school problems just might be related to a crush on a girl. And that, in turn, had brought back a slew of memories of her own.

She, too, had found it very hard to think about her schoolwork when she'd been involved with Joe, her first and only real love. Joe had also had trouble concentrating.

And unfortunately, it hadn't been just the two of them who'd noticed, Emma recollected ruefully, remembering Joe's high school wrestling coach. Coach Richards had resented her from the first time he'd seen her with Joe, and he'd made sure she knew it. She could still remember her most painful, humiliating run-in with Coach Richards. It had happened more than thirteen years before, yet she remembered their "talk" outside the gym that day as clearly as if it had happened yesterday....

"Emma Wilson, what are you doing here?" Coach Richards had asked when he'd found her outside the locker room, his displeasure evident. "School was over a long time ago. You should go home, girl. But then I suppose you know that, don't you?"

Her heart pounding, Emma held her books closer to her chest. She had never liked Coach Richards and she knew for a fact he didn't like her. She dreaded every run-in with him. And because she was Joe's girlfriend, and Joe was the star of his varsity wrestling team, they had plenty. Wetting her dry lips, she answered nervously, "I had to stay after to do some research in the library."

Coach Richards looked her up and down. "The library's at the other end of the school," he pointed out.

Emma flushed. There was no use pretending she didn't know that, or even, she reasoned dully, why she was here. Lifting her chin a little higher, she said, "I'm supposed to walk home with Joe."

Coach Richards scowled as he eyed her critically. "Yeah, well, Joe's got practice."

Coach Richards didn't run Joe's life, Emma reminded herself firmly. Nor did he run hers. Because he looked as if he expected her to run off, she said finally, "Joe asked me to meet him here. He said he would be done by five-thirty."

Coach's thin lips narrowed. "Yeah, well, he has to run laps in the gym today. Punishment. He couldn't keep his mind on what he was doing. You know of any reason why that would be?" Coach Richards prodded sarcastically as he scanned her slender form. He made her feel dirty and insignificant with a single lingering glance.

Not really wanting an answer from her, he continued, "Joe has a big match on Saturday, biggest of the year. If he wins, he'll go on to the state championships. And if he doesn't—" Joe's coach gave her a hard, accusing look "—well, we'll both know why, won't we, Emma?"

Emma had never wanted to be the reason Joe was robbed of his dreams; she loved him. Her eyes stinging with unshed tears, Emma turned wordlessly and started back down the hall. Joe's coach wanted her to leave. She'd leave. But she wouldn't go far, not when she knew Joe was still expecting to see her.

It was twenty-two degrees outside and a chill wind was blowing. Emma winced as the icy air hit her bare thighs and whipped up the hem of her pleated wool skirt. She ducked into a brick-walled nook beside the front windows of the school.

Joe came out of the school at six-fifteen, looking angry and disgruntled. Despite her wool knee socks and insulated gloves, Emma's fingers and toes were numb with the cold as she stepped out of the shadows.

"Emma!" Joe said. "What are you doing out here? It's dark and freezing. I've been looking all over the school for you."

Emma stepped into the warm circle of his arms. Moments before, she'd been depressed and guilty. No more. Whenever she was with Joe, all was well with the world. "I had a run-in with Coach Richards," she said, pressing her face against the hard muscles of his shoulder.

Joe frowned. Pulling back, he tucked his hand under her chin and lifted her face to his. "What'd he say?" His golden brown eyes searched hers anxiously.

Emma shrugged, hating to add to the burden of pressure Joe was under. "Nothing much," she lied. "He's just worried you don't have your mind on your wrestling."

Joe shook his head, clearly furious. He stalked away from her, every inch of him rigid with suppressed re-

sentment. "The guy just won't let up, will he?" Joe said, stomping closer once again. He looked down at Emma protectively, threatening darkly, "I've got half a mind to go back in and tell him off—"

"Joe, no," Emma interrupted, dreading the thought of another scene.

But Joe wasn't listening to her. "It isn't enough I've got my dad on my back all the time, now I've got Coach, too," he grumbled.

Emma knew how he felt and she empathized with him. She despised Joe's coach, too. He used personal attacks rather than good, fair coaching to control and spur on his team. If Joe didn't love the sport so much, the competition, she knew there was no way he would've put up with Coach's hassling. But Coach was right. Joe was almost to state. She couldn't, wouldn't stand in the way of that. And more important still, he needed his success on a varsity sport to help him get into the Naval Academy next fall.

The need for peace dictated her next move. "Let's just go home," she said, tucking her hand into his. Joe grumbled, but to Emma's relief, let her coax him into doing what she wanted and finally relented. They were almost to the end of the sidewalk along the front of the school, when Coach Richards's pickup pulled out of the lot. His headlights beamed on their figures, hand in hand. The truck screeched to a halt. Joe's coach got out, leaving his lights on, his engine running.

Ignoring Joe, Coach Richards looked straight at Emma. "I thought I'd explained to you, Emma, that Joe has to concentrate on his wrestling," he warned curtly.

Joe's face flushed angrily. "Don't talk to her that way!" he stormed, stepping slightly in front of Emma and shielding her body with his own tall, muscular form.

"Why not?" Coach Richards taunted. "It's God's truth. She'll be the ruin of you yet, Joe O'Reilly. And we're not just talking about the state wrestling championships, either. We're talking about the rest of your life, son. I've seen it happen so many times. You kids get too close. One thing leads to another and before you know it, you're dragged down into an early marriage, and when that happens, Joe, and it will," he prophesied heavily, "if the two of you continue on the same path, your dream of a career in the Navy will be nothing more than dust in the wind."

Tears spilled from Emma's lashes and fell heedlessly down her cheeks. "You're wrong," she protested emotionally, feeling as upset and angry with the coach as Joe looked. "I will never keep Joe from pursuing his dreams."

And in the end, she hadn't. Although Coach Richards, for all his bullying tactics, had been right—she would've given anything at the time if only she could have convinced Joe to stay... if only she could have married him instead of Skip.

His back to her, Joe continued to wade through junk, moving two old lamps and a radio that no longer worked, to uncover an old-fashioned linoleum-topped kitchen table. "So what do you think?" Joe asked. "Is a yard sale worthwhile?"

Jarred back to the present by his voice, Emma looked up from the box of books she'd been absently sorting through. "Yes," she said, steering her mind and her heart firmly away from the heartbreak of the past and back to the business at hand. "I think it'll be worthwhile. In fact, you can probably even get enough to cover the purchase of paint and wallpaper."

Joe screwed up his face comically. "Who'd want to buy this stuff?"

Emma returned confidently, "University students who need to furnish apartments as cheaply as possible. Skip can even put notices up on the bulletin boards over on campus." And if he wouldn't, she thought, she would.

Joe tensed at the mention of his ex-best friend's name. "I'd rather he not be involved in this."

Again, Emma felt like she was caught in a triangle. *Please, Joe, don't rock the boat anymore, don't throw us, even inadvertently, into crisis.* "Can't we all be friends again, Joe?"

"You and me, yes. Me and Skip, no," Joe said firmly, moving past her. "What's in those boxes behind you?"

Emma turned in the direction of his gaze. "I don't know," she said honestly, knowing just moments before she had wondered the same thing herself. "There's no marking on them—at least none I could see."

Joe nodded as he absorbed that information, then was quick to bark out orders, even as he was moving on to the far corner of the basement. "Take a look will you?" he called over his shoulder, lifting one well-toned leg over a two-shelf bookcase with a curiously psychedelic finish. "I want to see if I can get a look at this wardrobe over here."

As he moved stacks of Hardy Boys books, Emma shifted the boxes so she could get a look inside all of them simultaneously. The first was filled with tiny, old-fashioned toy soldiers made out of green plastic and several plastic tanks. She smiled as she realized these had obviously been Joe's toys when he was a child. Ditto for the next box, which held a Cubs cap and a Bears wall pennant.

"And, oh, look," Emma continued, verbally filling him in on contents of the various boxes as she went, "here's your old high school letter jacket and a National Honor Society gavel with your name engraved on it."

Grinning, Joe held out his hand. She carefully tossed him the gavel. He turned it over and over in his hand, his callused fingertips tracing the engraved letters. "Pounding this on the table was the best thing about being president of NHS."

"Power, hmm?" she teased.

Joe nodded affirmatively as his reminiscing smile broadened. "You got it." He jerked his head toward the box she was inspecting. "Anything else in there?"

Emma turned back to the box. "A little portfolio." As she picked it up, several papers fell out onto the floor. She cursed her own clumsiness. "Darn. Sorry." She bent to retrieve them and was stunned by what she saw—a photo of a young teenage girl, her resemblance to Joe unmistakable. Beneath the photo was an obituary. Her hands shaking with the impact of her discovery, Emma scanned the page. The words were faded and hard to read. Still, some leaped out at her.

"...sixteen...died Thursday...a student at Kansas City High School, preceded in death by her mother, Katie O'Reilly...survived by her father, Thomas William O'Reilly, and her brother, Joe..."

Emma's hand trembled even more as she stood up. This couldn't be, she thought, this just couldn't be.

"What is it?" he said, his voice becoming more alarmed as he took in her own shaken expression.

"It's an obituary for Mary O'Reilly."

He turned white. Anger glimmered in his golden brown eyes, and a wall went up between them. The muscles in his jaw clenched as he pushed heedlessly forward through the tide of discarded belongings to take the fragile piece of paper from her hand. "I didn't know that was down here," he said, stuffing it back into the portfolio. Taking possession of both, he turned away.

Silence fell between them, broken only by the pounding of Emma's heart. Frustration warred with the shock she felt. It was clear he planned to tell her nothing more. As if that would be acceptable to her! She couldn't believe, as close as they had once been, that he would never have told her about this. But he hadn't. "You had a sister?" she said, her voice strained.

Joe nodded tersely, his back to her. "She died in an accident when I was fourteen."

"I'm sorry," she said softly, meaning it, wishing there were some way she could make this easier for him. An only child, she had never had a sister or a brother, but she could imagine how much it must hurt to lose a sibling, and she grieved for Joe. Not just for what had happened, but for what he seemed unable to express.

"Yeah, well, I don't like to talk about it," he said gruffly, the forbidding look on his face preventing her from asking any more questions. "So where were we?"

I have no right to pry, Emma thought, getting his message to back off. Yet she was devastated nevertheless. She'd thought the two of them had shared everything, but how close could they have really been if Joe could have kept that from her? Had Coach Richards been right, she wondered on a new wave of humiliation and hurt. Had all she and Joe shared boiled down to one thing—an onslaught of teenage hormones? Was that all she had been to him, a convenient lay? Because if he had loved her, truly loved her... Even she and Skip shared practically everything. But Joe hadn't, not then, and it didn't look as if he would now, either.

And that in turn made her wonder with sharp disappointment how well she really knew Joe, how well anyone knew him. He had never talked much about what his life had been like before he moved to Evanston with his dad when he was fourteen.

Watching his rigid, retreating back, she wondered sadly if he ever would.

Chapter Five

The following afternoon, Bobby circled Emma incessantly, not speaking but not quite leaving her alone to work in peace and quiet, either. On his sixth aimless pass from the picture window in the living room to her desk and back again, she finally sighed and said, "Honey, please, could you stop your pacing? I'm trying to work out these papers on the Richfield closing, and I can't think with you doing that."

"Sorry, Mom," Bobby apologized immediately. His look expectant, he leaned genially against the corner of her desk. "I just gotta ask one question."

Emma looked up in anticipation, figuring it must be a doozy of a request if it had taken him this long to work up the courage to ask it. Even so, she was in no way prepared when he asked blithely, "Can I go next door and hang out for a while?"

"To the Harrises', you mean?"

"No. To Joe's."

Emma's heart faltered before resuming its normal beat. She swallowed hard around the tense knot of emotion that suddenly welled in her throat, trying hard not to think what this interest of Bobby's might mean. Or how Joe would react to the idea of having underfoot the child Emma and his ex-best friend had reared. Knowing the best way to handle this was with cool logic, she asked, "Why would you want to do that?"

"What do you mean, why?" Bobby repeated impatiently, looking as if he couldn't believe she was naive enough to ask such a thing. "There's a yard sale going on over there. Haven't you heard all the cars driving up and parking?"

That was part of the problem, Emma thought, as the tension in her throat moved downward, to her neck and then her shoulders. The car doors hadn't stopped opening and shutting all morning, and though she'd closed her windows to the commotion hours ago, she could still hear it inside the house, to distracting effect. She'd gone over the closing three times. The figures from the bank on their closing statement didn't match the figures she'd worked up earlier, but thus far she hadn't been able to concentrate well enough to discover precisely where the discrepancy came from. Until she did, there could be no closing as scheduled Monday morning.

"Honey, Joe's busy."

"I can help."

"He might not want you underfoot."

"Can I at least go and ask him if he *wants* me underfoot?"

Emma dismissed the idea with a single shake of her head. "Joe's too polite to say he doesn't."

"No, he isn't, Mom," Bobby argued back persuasively. "If he didn't want me over there, he'd just tell me so, real nice like."

Bobby was right, Emma thought. Joe would do exactly that and he'd do it without a qualm. He'd never had trouble speaking his mind, or telling people exactly what he wanted.

"Why don't you want me spending time with him?" Bobby continued, perplexed.

Because I'm afraid he'll realize what I did. Emma's hands started to shake. She was afraid that in some inadvertent, unconscious way Bobby would give them both away. And that she couldn't have.

She put her pen down. Her fingers still shook slightly, so she made a tight fist and hid them in her lap. "Don't you have some extra credit problems to do for algebra?" she asked. "To make up for all those homework assignments you didn't turn in?"

Bobby sulked. "Yes," he affirmed, making no move to go and do them.

Emma walked to the window and looked out. Joe was out in the yard, the warm May sun shining down on his dark hair. The goods in his yard were dwindling steadily. At the rate people were leaving with their arms full of purchases, Emma figured the sale couldn't go on more than a couple of hours. Inspired, she said, "I'll tell you what, Bobby. I'll make a deal with you. You finish your math and you can trot on over to Joe's."

Bobby's face lit up as if it was Christmas morning. "Deal!" he said, and dashed off.

Emma sighed and went back to her figures. An hour later she was sure the error was in the tax figures for the buyer. The bank had figured the taxes using a long proration, whereas she and her clients had figured them using a short proration, as agreed upon in the contract. It was an honest mistake, but one that would have to be worked out. She picked up the phone, intending to call the attorney handling the closing to let him know there was a problem. Bobby dashed in just as the attorney answered. He mouthed "I'm done" and ran out the door, slamming it behind him before she could admonish him to behave himself.

Three phone calls later, Emma had wrapped up her business for the day. The closing had been rescheduled for Wednesday, which would give them time to get new closing papers drawn up. Exhausted, she put her briefcase away and, curious about how Bobby was making out with Joe, went over to the window.

Joe was chatting it up with customers in his yard. Bobby sat behind the cashier's table, dutifully handling the exchange of goods and money. Watching the two of them working so well together, Emma couldn't help but wonder what it would have been like had she married Joe instead of Skip. Would Bobby have turned out the same way if Joe had reared him? Or would he have turned out less bookish and more of a man's man, like Joe? Would Bobby be in sixth grade now, instead of eighth, would he be playing sports and ruling the streets much as Joe had as a kid, instead of deliberately flunking algebra? There were no answers to those questions.

The last customer left. Emma looked down at her watch, and saw it was nearly 2:00 p.m. Feeling she should check up on Bobby to make sure he wasn't in Joe's way, she went out into the yard. "Hi. How's it going?" she said to Joe.

"Pretty good." Joe looked around in satisfaction. "We've sold almost everything worth anything. Whatever's left, I'm donating to the Salvation Army."

"Mom, did you see the punching bag and boxing gloves?"

Emma nodded, recalling how Joe had hung the bag from a tree in his backyard and boxed away at it on summer afternoons long ago. She didn't even have to close her eyes to remember what a beautiful body he had, sculpted with muscle, covered with smooth golden skin and a feathering of dark curly hair that arrowed down past his navel into the waistband of his pants. Lower still, he was every bit as beautiful and masculine.

"Yo, Mom! Wake up!"

Emma looked at Bobby, who was demanding her attention once again. A warm flush of color flowed into her cheeks.

"Joe says I can have the punching bag for free if I want, so can I?"

Having that bag around, and with it all the memories of the summer they had become lovers, might be more than she could handle. Emma looked at Joe. She wondered if he remembered, too, but there was no clue on his face. Only her own simmering passion to deal with. "You don't have to do that," she told him, ignoring the way her son's face fell in open disappointment.

"I want to do it," Joe said firmly with a friendly smile. His eyes held hers and probed deeply. "I wouldn't have offered it to him if I didn't." As she considered the puzzled look on his ruggedly handsome face, Emma could tell he wondered why it should be so difficult for her to accept such a gift from him. After all, it was for Bobby, not for her.

Struggling to subdue her disappointment—he didn't remember, after all—she looked back at her son. One glance at his young face told her Bobby would be crushed if she didn't allow it. "All right," she said finally, with obvious reluctance, "but it goes in the basement, not in your room." *Where I won't have to see it or be reminded.*

"All right!" Bobby jumped up from the table to slap palms with Joe in reciprocal high fives. "Can I go try it out now?"

"Sure," Joe said. "Just go easy with the punches at first. I don't want you hurting your hand."

Bobby tore off, bag and gloves in tow.

Emma faced Joe awkwardly. "It was nice of you to let Bobby hang out here this afternoon," she said. She and Joe were alone now in the sunny yard, the fragrant May breeze stirring all around them.

"I enjoyed it. He's a great kid," Joe said quietly.

Hand to her spine, he led her over to the lawn chairs he'd set up behind the cashier's table. Reaching around him, he produced a thermos bottle and poured her a capful of icy lemonade. Emma took it wordlessly and sipped until she'd had her fill. He drained what was left in the cup, poured himself a little more and drained that, too.

"So, did you get your real estate papers all worked out? Bobby said you had some trouble with some figures."

Emma nodded, wishing she weren't so aware of him. Maybe if the years hadn't been so kind... But they had been, and when she looked at him she couldn't help but note how age had added a rugged masculinity to the chiseled bones of his face that would have been hard for any woman to ignore. His golden brown eyes reflected a wisdom beyond his years. His mouth seemed even wider and more sensual than she remembered it.

He was still waiting for an answer. As if business was all she had on her mind, Emma replied, "There's a mistake in the figures the mortgage company worked up that's thrown a wrench in the closing scheduled for Monday morning."

"Bad news for the client," he sympathized, still watching her curiously, as if he half suspected something else was up.

Emma shrugged and studied the well-trimmed yard of the neighbor across the street. "It'll delay things for a few days, but that's all." She reached down and picked a speck of imaginary lint from the knee of her tailored white linen slacks. "It occasionally happens. That's why we double-check everything so we can find it if and when it does happen."

"You're good at what you do," he observed, watching as she nervously flattened her palm and smoothed the fabric over her knee.

"Yes."

"And you like it?"

He really is interested, Emma thought, feeling oddly pleased despite herself. "Yes, I do," she admitted in the same honest vein, relieved to talk with Joe about something else besides the triangle of him, herself and Skip. Her hand stilling its nervous motions, she looked into Joe's eyes. "It was difficult at first, building up a clientele. Now I get more referrals than I can handle sometimes."

"It's easy to see why," Joe returned casually. "You're still as efficient and responsible and hard-working as ever."

She paused, glad he hadn't said what for one brief, insane moment she'd thought he was going to say, that she was still as beautiful as ever. Because even though, from a strictly feminine viewpoint, she wanted Joe and indeed every man she had known years ago to think that, it would have demeaned her if he had said so. It would have made it seem as if he thought she was getting by on her looks, when that wasn't what she did at all.

Aware she'd stayed far longer than she initially planned, Emma stood. "Thank you for being so kind to Bobby."

"No problem."

"About the bag and the gloves—I should pay you something."

"Forget it," he advised with a gentle smile. "But, if you want to reciprocate . . ." He gave her a hopeful smile.

Emma had never been able to resist Joe when he was at his most vulnerable.

"You could go with me to the paint and carpet store," Joe continued, "and help me make the best selections, since I don't know anything about either." He gestured in the direction of her redecorated home. "And you obviously do."

As his real estate agent, she would benefit if he painted the house in the most salable colors, Emma reasoned. Putting aside the latent discomfort she felt whenever she was around him for any length of time, Emma asked crisply, "When would you want to go?"

"This evening, say around six?" Joe paused as if the actual time were of no consequence to him. "We could take Bobby along."

Emma wasn't sure that was a good idea; she only knew it wouldn't be possible. "Bobby and Skip have already made plans to go to a movie." And he was spending the night with Skip afterward. "But I could go."

"You don't have a date or anything?" Joe pressed.

She had an idea what he was thinking. It was Saturday night. She was single. "No," she said simply, trying hard not to notice the satisfied smile that followed her announcement.

"I guess it's just you and me, then," he said, not bothering to hide his pleasure at the easy way things were working out. "Six-thirty?"

Emma nodded. This wasn't a date, or anywhere near it, she told herself firmly. Just two old friends trying to help each other out. "I'll be ready."

"So WHERE do you want to go?" Joe asked after Emma had met him in his driveway and they'd both climbed into his Jeep. As he had expected, Emma didn't hesitate to tell him what she thought best.

"There's a new decorating warehouse in Waukegan," she suggested in a forthright tone, her demeanor proper and professional. "Some of my clients have used it, with great results. If you don't mind the drive, we could go there."

Twenty or so miles up there, twenty or so miles back, Joe figured. That would give them some time to talk, time when Emma couldn't run away from him. He wanted that more than he probably should, maybe because she'd seemed a little high-strung since he'd been back, relaxed and friendly one minute, visibly hurt the next, nervous—for no reason he could figure—the next. He wanted to know why. He sometimes got the feeling she was hiding something.

But right now, they had to concentrate on the paint and carpet. Understanding her again...that would also come, he hoped. "Show me the way," he said.

Emma gave him directions, and off they went. As he drove north, Joe realized it felt good having her beside him in his Jeep, even if she wasn't being as talkative as usual. Of course he knew why she wasn't, too. She was still disappointed in him because he wouldn't talk about his sister, but he was sure he was doing the right thing in leaving that a closed subject.

He knew from bitter experience that talking about his pain, his rage, over Mary's death only intensified the hurt. He didn't want to remember that he had blamed his dad for what had happened, or that, even now, he still felt her death could easily have been avoided. He just wanted it to never have happened. He wanted not to dwell on it. Just the way Emma wanted not to dwell on or even discuss her reasons for hastily marrying Skip. To stay locked in the past would be to become bitter forever, and that he didn't want. And neither did Emma, he was sure.

Once inside the paint warehouse, Emma told him what she had in mind.

"You want to do the whole house in beige?" he asked, unable to completely hide his incredulity. "Beige carpets? Beige walls?" Beige everything?

"It's bone, and yes, I think that'd be best," Emma insisted stubbornly, holding her ground.

"Isn't that kind of dull?"

Emma smiled. "On the contrary. Neutral colors provide a soothing background and make the house ready to move in, and hence more salable. People with any color or style of furniture can feel comfortable moving right in. On the other hand, say you decided to paint the walls oyster blue and the potential buyers have orange and purple furniture—"

"I don't know if I want to sell to anyone with orange and purple furniture," Joe interrupted, not sure why he was giving her such a hard time.

Emma took a deep breath and started again, her tone patient. "Okay, say they have a green-and-lavender color scheme."

She was so serious. Joe couldn't help teasing her a little. "Ditto the green and lavender." He shook his head regretfully. "Sorry, I just can't sell to anyone with furniture like that. Imagine what would happen to the neighborhood if I did. Hell, they might even put birdbaths on the front lawn," he whispered in a scandalized tone, liking the way her blue eyes lit up and the pink color poured into her fair cheeks when she started to get mad.

Eyeing him facetiously, Emma put her hands on her hips. Joe noted that she looked more alive than she had all evening. "Are you giving me a hard time?" she demanded, wordlessly daring him to keep it up.

"Looks that way, doesn't it?" he returned dryly. Then, because he felt he'd yanked her chain enough, he continued with an easy grin before she could protest again. "I get your point," he reassured her in a soft, unintentionally lazy tone, "so beige—er, bone—it is."

For a moment Emma said nothing, merely looked into his eyes, as if trying to determine whether bone was the color he really wanted or if he was just going along because he didn't want to make a decision himself. Reminded suddenly of the way she had always been able to read his mind, to dig down and find his vulnerability and minister to it, Joe looked back at her and realized something else. He had missed her all these years; he was just beginning to discover how much. Maybe because no one had ever challenged him and piqued and understood him quite the way Emma had. Nor was he sure anyone else ever would.

There was no telling how long they would have stood that way, locked in silent, wordless reverie, if a salesperson had not walked up and interrupted. "Newlyweds, aren't you?" the clerk in the sharkskin suit assumed smoothly.

Joe was about to set the man straight when he saw the astonished look on Emma's face. He turned to the clerk. "You could tell that right off?"

"Oh, yes," the clerk responded with utter, misplaced confidence. "Just one look at the two of you and I knew. I said to myself, now there's a couple who's serious about making a home *their home*. I could tell right off by the way you were looking at each other."

Because Emma seemed to be withdrawing into herself again, Joe teased, "We look that devoted to each other, hmm?"

Emma sent him a cool amused look for playing along, but he noticed she made no immediate move to correct the clerk's mistaken assumption, either. "Or that argumentative," she said drolly. She turned to the clerk. "Joe wasn't sure about the colors I selected."

"Did I say that?" Joe interrupted.

"No, but you were thinking it," Emma countered.

"Now, now, there's no need to argue," the clerk intervened smoothly. "I'm sure if we put our heads together we can all come to some agreement."

"I'm sure we can, too," Joe said, deadpan. "Isn't that right, honey?" He was immediately rewarded with an amused, slightly mischievous glint in Emma's clear blue eyes.

"I'm sure we can, too, sweetheart," she said, mocking his tone to a T before surprising him by amending imperiously, "as long as we do it my way."

Aware she had just taken control of the farce he'd created, Joe faced her in mock indignation. The one thing he had always loved about Emma was her sheer unpredictability.

"Now wait just a minute, honeybunch," he countered firmly, determined to regain the upper hand. "This is my house we're talking about here." Out of the corner of his eye, Joe saw the clerk fairly wince.

Emma tossed her head. "And my good taste is needed to make it presentable."

Joe palmed his chest. "Aren't you forgetting something? Since I'm paying for it—" Joe saw the clerk wince again at Joe's outdated attitude "—I have the final say."

Emma turned so only he could see the mischief in her eyes. "Then why'd you even bother to ask me along?" she demanded.

"Now, folks, please." The clerk stepped between them, beads of sweat visible on his brow. "Let's just cool our tempers, shall we?"

Joe looked into Emma's eyes for a long time. The last thing he wanted was to cool down when the two of them were so in sync, but maybe it was time they let the presumptuous clerk off the tenterhooks he'd been hanging on the past few minutes. Aware she was trying hard not to smile, too, he released a long breath and said, in feigned defeat, "All right. You win, honeycakes. The beige it is."

Emma handed the clerk the specifications. All too relieved to get away from the marital bickering, the clerk ran off to do an estimate. Alone with Joe beside the carpet samples, Emma chuckled. "We shouldn't have done that, Joe."

"Yeah, I know."

"It was immature of us."

"And fun." And from the look of her, Emma didn't have fun very often anymore. No, her life was all duty and responsibility. Much as his had been.

At Joe's remark, she withdrew a bit. Turning, she cast a glance at the desk where the clerk was busy working. "Poor guy," she said softly. "He really thinks we're married."

We wanted to be, Joe thought. But if Emma was thinking—wishing—the same thing, she didn't show it. He studied her pale cheeks, wondering what had made her pull away from him like that, just when they were starting to get close enough to joke around again. "I take it marriage doesn't appeal to you?" he probed softly, after a moment, wanting to know what had her so down.

Emma shook her head, looking more tense. "No, not since I was married to Skip." Avoiding his glance, she rushed on, murmuring what seemed to Joe to be the first thing that came to her mind. "I wonder what made him think we were married."

Hating the emotional wall Emma had just thrown up between them, for no reason he could see, Joe shrugged. "Lots of things, probably. We're about the same age. And there was our body language," Joe continued when Emma continued to regard him with that same perplexed, not entirely pleased, look. "We were standing fairly close together while we studied the paint chips." Close enough for him to inhale the fragrant, flowery scent of her hair and skin. Close enough for him to remember the way it had once been between them. Emma was always so warm and giving and sensual. He wondered if she still made love with such abandon, or if the years had changed that about her, too.

She wasn't the same these days. She was confident now, independent almost to a fault, withholding as much as she gave. She deliberately held him at a distance these days, keeping her vulnerability well hidden. It was almost as if she was afraid of him sometimes, the way she looked at him. Why, he couldn't fathom. He hadn't hurt her. She'd hurt him. Was that it—was she fearing some sort of retribution on his part?

He turned back to her. Emma was still looking at the samples they'd selected. "The house is really going to look nice," she said.

The house would look brand-new when he'd finished with it. To his surprise, Joe began to see it might not be as easy to leave Evanston—and Emma—again as he'd thought. He pushed aside the notion of staying. The only practical solution was selling the house, especially considering how he still felt about Emma. Desiring her, yet not quite trusting her. Forgiving her, and yet not. It still wasn't easy to see her with Skip, and because of Bobby, she was with Skip all the time.

The clerk returned.

While Emma waited patiently for him to decide, Joe looked at the figures and found them acceptable.

Again, he had an idea what it would be like to be married to Emma. And that made him distinctly uncomfortable. He had to stop fantasizing about a future with Emma, a home here in Evanston again, because it could never be. He was married to the Navy now, Joe reminded himself, and he loved every damn minute of it.

He looked at the clerk, suddenly as anxious to get back to his real life as the clerk was to make a sale. "When will this be ready?"

"YOU DON'T have to help me carry the paint into the garage."

"Don't be silly, Joe," Emma said as she followed him into his garage. She wasn't sure why he was in a bad mood. At the carpet and paint store he'd turned remote and grumpy, and had been so ever since, despite her attempts to be pleasant and sociable. "You've got twenty gallons here. That'd be ten trips."

"If you carry two at a time," he corrected, muscles bunching as he lifted the heavy cans from the back of his car. "I can carry four."

He didn't have to remind her how strong he was. She knew from experience how it felt to be wrapped in his arms, and held against him, length to length.

But she didn't want to think about that. She stuck her tongue out at him playfully. "Show off."

He laughed. "You show off, too."

"Oh, yeah," she challenged good-naturedly, "when?"

Joe didn't have to think long to come up with an example. "Every time you beat someone at gin rummy," he pointed out solemnly, "you get a certain very wicked, very triumphant glint in your eye."

He knew so many things about her, Emma thought. No wonder the clerk at the decorating-supply warehouse had thought they were married! She'd felt as if they were a couple as they shopped. It would be so easy to slip back into the relationship—physically, nothing had changed. She still got breathless when she was around him. Emotionally, she was even more attracted to him; he understood her inner vulnerability and the reason for it better than anyone. But he wouldn't understand her deception and lies, her betrayal of them both. Recalling that, she realized she couldn't get any closer to Joe.

"Looks like you've got your work cut out for you this week," she remarked, thinking gratefully that he'd be so busy he wouldn't have time to give her those heavy-lidded, deeply sensual looks.

Joe nodded happily, reminding Emma that he had never been opposed to hard work but rather had enjoyed it immensely, especially the physical tasks.

Joe looked at Emma, saw she was reluctant to leave and realized suddenly he didn't want her to go, either. Not yet. Not when he knew they had so little time together and that in all likelihood, after he left Evanston this time, he would never see her again. "So, want to keep me company while I paint tomorrow?" he asked casually, thinking there would be no harm in that.

He wants to pick up where we left off, she thought, but she knew better than anyone why she couldn't let that happen. "I'm sorry, Joe, but I've got an open house to go to tomorrow afternoon."

Joe swallowed his disappointment. "Right." He'd been a fool to think they could just be friends, or that she would even want to be. She was selling his house, that was all.

"But I've got an idea." She smiled at him brightly, surprising him with her enthusiasm. "You could have a painting party. That way it wouldn't be so lonely for you and you'd get the house in shape to sell a lot sooner, too." And the sooner his house sold, the sooner they could both go back to their normal lives, Emma reasoned. She could stop worrying about him uncovering the real reason behind her hasty ill-fated marriage to Skip. She could stop worrying she'd fall in love with Joe all over again, and in doing so, tear apart the very fabric of all their lives.

As Joe continued to regard her intently, she saw a flash of hurt in his eyes. "Sure," he said with forced enthusiasm. "A painting party would be great."

Chapter Six

The painting party was in full swing next door when Emma got home from the open house at five-thirty. Feeling a little left out, and knowing there was no reason for it, she went on into her house and found it was as silent as Joe's was noisy. On the kitchen table, she found a note. "Emma, Bobby and I are next door. We'll see you later, around seven or so. Love, Skip."

Skip was next door at the painting party? And he had Bobby with him? Emma thought incredulously.

She traded her business suit for jeans and a sweatshirt, and headed over to Joe's. Inside were many of the people who had been at Joe's Welcome Home party the previous week. All were working hard. The air was filled with the sounds of music, talk and laughter, and scented with the smell of new paint.

"Hi, Mom!" Bobby yelled from the living room where he was carefully rolling gleaming lines of bone paint onto the wall.

She smiled and picked her way carefully to his side, being careful not to trip on the many drop cloths and newspapers laid out to protect the floor from spatters. "Hi, honey. Where's your dad?"

"Last I saw, he was painting one of the bedrooms," Bobby reported excitedly. "Are you going to paint, too?"

Emma's heart stalled in her chest as she thought of the possibility of working side by side next to Joe. Or worse, watching some other woman work next to him. "I don't know," she answered honestly. "It depends on if I'm needed or not." Right now, from what she could tell, it seemed they were almost done.

Picking her way through the drop cloths and paint cans, Emma said hi to everyone and made her way to the bedrooms. Skip was in the last one. He looked happy to see her. "You got my note, I guess."

Emma nodded as she wondered what was really going on here. Had Skip and Joe buried the hatchet? "Joe invited you?" she probed casually, knowing she had to find out how this had all come about.

Skip put down his brush and wiped his hands on the white hand towel he'd tucked into the waistband of his jeans. "Surprised me, too, when he called." He paused, looking her up and down, focusing at last on the heightened color in her cheeks. "What's been going on? Have you been urging him to extend the olive branch?"

Yes, Emma thought, *but I didn't think he was listening.* "Of course I have. I want us all to be friends again. So does Doris. I'm glad you and Joe are on speaking terms now."

Skip squinted at the ceiling and made no comment, leading Emma to think there was still a lot simmering beneath the surface of both men's emotions. "Want to help me out here?" Skip asked.

Emma speculated how Joe would react if he found her and Skip working side by side in his house, then how Skip would react if he saw her working side by side with Joe. Deciding the tenuous peace was worth holding on to, she decided to seek out a safe harbor. "Maybe in a minute," she said evasively, already backing out the door. "I want to say hello to Doris first. She's here, isn't she?" If anyone could tell her what was going on, if there really was peace between the two men, it was Doris.

Skip gave her a hard, assessing look, but said only, "Last I saw she was in the kitchen."

Doris wasn't in the kitchen; Joe was. He looked up from the tray of sandwiches he was uncovering as she came in. He had specks of bone-colored paint in his dark hair and trailing down one cheek. More paint was speckled across the Navy sweatshirt covering his broad chest. His jeans were old and tight, the edges of the seams frayed and white. They gloved the flatness of his abdomen and his long muscled thighs, and tapered down his calves to his ankles. Reminded of the coiled strength in his hips and legs, of how it had felt to be braced up against them, Emma felt tension curl in her abdomen and just as determinedly pushed it away.

"Hey, Emma." Joe offered her a lazy smile and the full impact of his mesmerizing golden brown eyes. "How was the open house?"

"Okay." Looking into his face, she could tell that despite the gritty nature of what he knew he'd be do- ing all day, he had still taken the time to shave and shower that morning. His short brown hair was rumpled and getting longer.

"What?" Joe prodded without preamble.

She ignored the thrill of excitement that rushed up her spine every time she was alone with him. Swallowing around the sudden tension in her throat, she protested softly, keeping her eyes level with his, "I didn't say anything."

"I know, but you're thinking something. I can see that brain of yours going a hundred miles a minute." His gaze narrowed speculatively. He dropped what he was doing and stepped nearer. "So what is it?"

Emma had to fight the urge to draw back. "I saw Skip."

"Yeah, it was nice of him to help out." Joe kept his eyes on hers and it was all she could do not to squirm, step back, put some sort of anesthetizing distance between them.

I'm here. I might as well find out what's going on. "He said you asked him."

Joe nodded, briefly looking as if he felt a little troubled about that. Emma was reminded how much he hated pretense of any kind.

Moving closer, Emma whispered, "I didn't think you wanted to become friends with Skip again." And vice versa.

Joe shrugged. "I changed my mind."

Emma didn't trust this sudden about-face. Joe was as stubborn as they came. "Why?"

Wordlessly, he took her hand and led her out the back door and around to the side of the house. She let him lead her because she didn't want their conversation overheard, either. "You think I have an ulterior motive, inviting him here?"

"I don't know," she said evenly. "That's why I'm asking. Do you?"

Joe let out his breath slowly. "Yes," he said, his frustration with her questions evident. "I do. You've made it very clear you want me to patch things up with Skip. For that matter, so does everyone else in our circle of friends here. They seem to think bygones should be just that. So, for your sake," he said heavily, "for mine, I'm willing to try."

Emma sagged against the wall, aware how close he was. "Thank you," she said quietly. She had an idea how much this was costing him, and she was grateful to him for trying. Just as she was grateful to Skip for accepting Joe's tentative offer of peace. Feeling suddenly shy and all too aware of him, she ducked her head and stared at the grass between their shoes. "I don't like feeling caught between the two of you."

"I know that. And believe it or not, Emma, as angry as I was with you all these years, it was never my intention to come back here and make your life hell," Joe said.

"What? No fantasies of revenge?" she teased.

"I don't work that way and you know it."

"I know," Emma admitted quietly. "The whole situation has been very difficult." *For both of us.*

"Maybe now it will start to get easier," Joe said, reaching over to take her hand in his and stroke it lightly, reassuringly.

Emma tilted her head back to better see his face. Warmth was spiraling through her at a dangerous rate.

"I hope so," she said softly. She wanted to be close to Joe again, so much. And as his head lowered slowly, inexorably to hers, she had the strong sensation he wanted it, too.

The next thing she knew he had his free hand beneath her chin, was tilting it back. His other hand was lacing through her hair. His mouth was lowering. Her heart slammed against her ribs in anticipation of his kiss and her lips were parting. She knew they shouldn't be doing this, and yet...and yet she wanted to feel his mouth on hers again, searching and igniting. She wanted to be held against his warm strong body and to feel his arms encircle and hold her close. She wanted to lose herself in the rapacious intensity of his golden brown eyes. And lower still, lower still...she wanted...

The back door slammed, acting like a bucket of ice water on her tense, yearning body.

"Funny—" they both heard Doris say as they jerked apart guiltily, in much the same way they had when they were kids when one of their fathers had caught them kissing. *I didn't expect to feel this way with him,* Emma thought as she lost her battle against an involuntary flush. She was older now, independent, and yet around him she was as vulnerable and seeking as a lovesick teenager.

"—I could've sworn I saw Emma come out this way. Oh!" Doris said as she rounded the corner unexpectedly. "There you are."

To Emma's chagrin, Skip was right behind her. Anger flashed in his eyes as he saw the flushed, guilty looks on their faces, quickly followed by hurt. Thankfully, Emma thought, as heat moved over her in undulating waves, Doris was quick to recover. "We were wondering if you wanted to take a dinner break now. The crew's getting pretty hungry." In an effort to break the tension, Doris laughed a little too jovially and patted her trim middle, adding, "Or at least I am."

Skip's lips clamped together in abject disapproval as his gaze roved over Emma from head to toe, then turned on Joe. "I'm out of paint," Skip announced coolly. "I didn't see any more in the living room."

"It's in the garage," Joe said casually, recovering from their near embrace faster than Emma could ever hope to. "C'mon, I'll show you." He led Skip around the front, while Emma and Doris slipped in the back. "So what's going on with the two of you?" Doris asked the moment they were alone.

"Nothing," Emma replied, hating the defensive edge that had crept, unbidden, into her voice. She made herself smile and pretend she wasn't abysmally disappointed at the interruption. "We were just talking." *And trying to work in a kiss. Or two. Or three.*

Doris's brows lifted skeptically. "Uh-huh. It looked like more than that to me. It looked like he was about to kiss you."

Emma recalled the sensation of his lips so close to hers, the compelling warmth and gentleness of his hands. Part of her wanted him so very much, if only to see if the passion they'd once felt still existed. But there were so many reasons why that could never be. Joe would never forgive her if he found out what she and Skip had done to him. She couldn't forget that,

Emma reminded herself sternly. She had Bobby to consider. And herself and Skip.

"So you've been here all afternoon?" Emma asked Doris, struggling to appear casual as Doris opened packages of paper plates and she pulled cold salads out of the fridge.

"Yep," Doris said, friend enough to let the subject of Emma's near kiss with Joe drop. "So how's the search for a buyer for this place coming?" she continued casually as she pulled the lids off fruit and potato salad.

Emma was relieved to switch the subject to business. "It isn't. The house hasn't been listed yet," Emma confided. Briefly, she explained the reasons for the delay.

"I see your point," Doris said after listening intently. "It probably will sell faster once it's fixed up. You don't mind if I go ahead and put out word at the station, though, do you? I know several people who are in the process of looking for a house."

"That'd be great," Emma said. She touched her hair and discovered it was tousled. Smoothing the ends self-consciously, she continued with forced practicality, "I know Joe wants to sell it as soon as possible, preferably before he leaves." And, as much as part of her would hate to see Joe go, Emma acknowledged sadly, she knew it was best. There were still too many secrets. Secrets that had to be kept.

"BOBBY, IT'S TIME for supper," Emma called the following evening.

When she got no response, she went back to his room and glanced in.

What she saw alarmed her. Bobby was doubled over on his bed, both arms clutching his stomach. A sheen of sweat glistened on his face; beneath it, the skin was green.

"Honey, what's wrong?" Emma asked, beginning to panic as she knelt down beside him. She'd never seen him in so much pain!

He moaned. "Ohhh, it . . . hurts . . . Mom."

"How long have you been this way?" Emma asked. He'd come home from school an hour ago, muttering something about homework and had gone straight to his room. She hadn't thought anything about it—these days, he always had a lot of homework.

Bobby shrugged in answer to her question and a single tear rolled down his cheek. Emma felt his forehead. Despite the sweat on his face, his skin was cool to the touch, which meant no fever. Could it be appendicitis? All Emma knew for sure was that she had to get him to the emergency room. And judging from the state he was in, there was no time to spare. "Hang on, honey," she said, "I'm going to call your doctor."

Unfortunately, their family physician had already left his office for the day. His service promised her they would get her message to him as soon as possible and in the meantime advised her to take Bobby to the hospital where he was on staff. Knowing she couldn't get Bobby out to the car alone—he was much too heavy for her and in no shape to walk—she tried Skip, but he wasn't home, yet, either. In desperation, she dialed Joe's number. He picked up on the third ring. Quickly, she explained the problem.

To her relief, he was at her door in two minutes flat. She'd never been so glad to see anyone in her life. "Where is he?" Joe asked, his golden eyes as worried as her own.

"In his bedroom. C'mon." Briskly, Emma led the way.

"Joe!" Bobby protested weakly between spasms of pain. "What are you doing here?"

Joe knelt down beside him. Sliding one strong arm beneath Bobby's shoulders, another beneath his knees, he prepared to scoop her son up into his arms. "We're going to take you to the hospital, buddy."

"No!" Bobby's face flooded with riotous color. He pushed at Joe's shoulders and roused himself enough to sit up.

His defiance shocked them both. Emma turned to Bobby. "Honey, you're sick," she said.

"No, I'm not." Bobby's eyes slid away. Emma saw her son's misery and his guilt and knew immediately he'd been up to something. The question was what. She and Joe exchanged a look.

"Mom, I know what it is." Bobby pushed the words out through gritted teeth. "I ate . . . twenty-five jalapeño peppers." He sniffed. "On a dare, after school! And don't yell at me, Mom," he admonished, covering both his ears with his hands and ducking his head in shame. "I already feel bad enough!"

Emma could see that. She looked at Joe. "Maybe we still should take him to the emergency room."

In the background, the phone rang. "That's probably our family doctor now," Emma said, dashing off to get it.

She was right in her assumption. Quickly, she explained to their doctor what had happened. He assured her it wasn't serious—Bobby's stomach was just letting him know in no uncertain terms never to do this again—and advised her to give him a dose of antacid.

Bobby swallowed the chalky liquid obediently, then lay back against the pillows. Gradually, as the antacid worked, he began to relax. Joe sat next to him, talking to him gently and sponging Bobby's face with a damp cloth from time to time.

Emma sat at the foot of his bed. She was glad Joe was there. And she wasn't. It was hard, seeing the two of them this way, because it reminded her of all that might have been had she just waited for Joe to graduate from the academy, instead of running off and foolishly marrying his best friend.

After several moments, Joe cocked his head. "Do I smell something burning?"

"Oh my gosh, dinner!" Emma said. Leaving Joe to stay with Bobby, she dashed off to rescue the pot of green beans that had boiled dry on the stove. By the time she'd turned off the oven and returned to Bobby's room, the two were deep in conversation. She could tell by the low confidential tones—so different from the casual conversation of before—that this was an intensely private, man-to-man exchange. Not wanting to interrupt, she paused mid-hall.

"Look, I know how you feel, Bob," Joe was saying, "it's hard *not* to take a dare—"

"They've been calling me a sissy all year, ever since all the other guys started growing and got so much taller than me," Bobby confided. "I figured if I showed them I wasn't they'd leave me alone, stop pushing me into the lockers and stuff."

Joe was silent a moment, taking that in. As was Emma. She hadn't known Bobby had been getting a rough time from the other guys at school. He hadn't said a thing to her. But then maybe he couldn't, she thought. Maybe he'd been too embarrassed. "Did it work?" Joe asked.

"I don't know," Bobby said desultorily after a minute. "They sure seemed impressed. No one thought I could do it. They all figured I'd stop after the first pepper, or the second or the third. But I showed them, didn't I, Joe?"

Oh, Bobby, Emma thought, dismayed, tears of empathy for what her son had been through streaming down her face. *Don't you know friends like that aren't worth winning?*

"Let me tell you a story, Bobby, about someone who was very close to me," Joe responded in a low and contemplative voice, and though Emma couldn't see his face from where she was standing, she could imagine the gentleness of his look and was glad Bobby was able to talk to him.

"She didn't make friends very easily and she wanted to prove herself, too. So when she was about your age she started doing all sorts of crazy stuff. At first it was just a little shoplifting, then some chug-a-lug contests with some beer they got from an older friend. She didn't get caught at any of it and it all seemed pretty harmless, you know?''

Yes, Emma did know about things like that. She didn't know who Joe was talking about though.

"What happened?" Bobby asked curiously.

"Well, she got real popular," Joe said. "She was invited to all the best parties at school."

"See?" Emma heard Bobby say, as if that just proved his case. She clamped her hand to her mouth, so he wouldn't hear her disappointed sigh.

Heedless of Bobby's emotional interruption, Joe continued patiently, "Then one night she and some of her daredevil friends went out to this old railroad bridge. They'd all been drinking a little bit. They decided it would be fun to walk across it. So they started walking, one by one. She was dead center of the bridge when the train came, Bob." Joe's voice broke a little. Even though the length of the hallway and the wall to Bobby's room separated them, Emma could feel the iron will it took for Joe to continue.

"She tried to jump out of the way, but there'd been a drought that summer and the water in the river wasn't very deep. She hit bottom and broke her neck."

Utter silence. Emma felt more tears roll down her cheek. She wasn't sure why she was crying. Part of it was relief—she was glad Bobby was okay. Part of it was empathy for the pain Bobby and Joe both had apparently been through.

"Were you walking on the bridge, too?" Bobby asked after a moment in a very subdued voice.

"No," Joe said sadly. "I wasn't there that night. By that time I'd stopped hanging around with her because I didn't like her new friends. But I'll tell you something, Bob." Again, his voice broke. "I wish I had been. 'Cause if I'd been there, I wouldn't have let her take that stupid dare."

"You're trying to tell me not to be such a jerk next time, aren't you?" Bobby said in a low quavering voice.

Joe retorted gently, "Yep. I like you, kid, and I don't want to see you get hurt."

Bobby sighed loud and long. "Yeah, well, don't worry, I won't ever eat peppers again."

"One or two would be okay," Joe was quick to allow.

Bobby groaned. "The way I'm feeling, even the smell of one would be too much."

Joe laughed softly. "Close your eyes. Get a little rest. I'll be back to check on you in a few minutes."

Joe met up with her in the hall. One glance at the stricken look on her face and he knew she had heard everything. Together, not speaking, they headed for the kitchen at the opposite end of the house. Once they were alone, the moment only got more awkward. Emma was touched he had shared such an intimate part of his life with Bobby, and hurt that he hadn't told her sooner. To cover the onslaught of feelings, she asked, "I've pretty much killed the green beans, but the meat loaf, tossed salad and scalloped potatoes are still alive and well, so if you'd like to stay and eat with me—"

Joe shook his head. "Thanks for the invitation. It sounds delicious, but I already ate."

Emma tried not to feel too disappointed.

"I'm sorry I got you over here like this," she continued matter-of-factly. "But I was in such a panic. And I couldn't reach Bobby's doctor or Skip—"

"That's okay. All I was doing was painting baseboard."

For the first time, Emma noticed Joe's plain gray sweatpants and a matching sweatshirt. There was no paint on his face or in his hair this time, but it was on his hands—specks and smudges of gleaming white paint.

She swallowed, continuing, "He really scared me."

Joe acknowledged her fear with an understanding jerk of his head, adding, "He scared himself."

Again, the silence stretched out between them. Emma wanted to talk to him about what she'd overheard, but she could also see he wasn't about to broach the subject himself. Same old Joe, she thought with frustration. He had always kept his most private pain to himself. And always would. Whereas she, knowing a burden was less heavy when conceded to, just looked for someone to share it with. Maybe there were some secrets they were destined to take with them to their graves, but not this, she thought. "I heard what you told him about losing a friend."

Joe's jaw turned rigid. Suddenly, he got the same haunted look in his eyes that he'd had when she'd found the clipping about his sister's death, the sister he never talked about. And abruptly Emma knew. "The girl you told Bobby about was your sister, wasn't she, Joe?"

Joe nodded.

And yet you never told me about her, Emma thought, hurt.

"I don't know why I brought Mary's story up," Joe said. "Except because I thought maybe it would help Bobby."

Because she sensed how difficult this was for him, Emma was quiet, waiting.

He watched her, his face immobile, then pulled a chair out and sat facing the back, his arms hooked over the top, his legs straddling the seat. Having come to some inner decision, he continued, "She was never the same after my mother died when we were kids."

Emma nodded her comprehension. "It's hard being a girl, growing up without a mother. There are things like hair and makeup and clothes and boys that you just can't go to a father about. At least not in those days," she sighed, hoping that today it was different.

"I know," Joe agreed. "Mary felt the same way. And it got worse when she entered junior high. She was just so angry that she didn't have a mother. And my dad, instead of setting her straight and letting her know how much she had to be thankful for, made all kinds of excuses for her behavior. He refused to lay down the law to her—even though he had no trouble doing so for me—and she just got wilder and wilder. I knew something like that might happen, but kept thinking, hoping, that she'd come to her senses. But she didn't."

"It's not your fault, Joe." None of it was. He'd been little more than Bobby's age when his sister had died, yet it was clear from the tormented look on his face that he blamed himself.

He pushed away from the chair and strode to the window overlooking her backyard. He shoved his hands in his back pockets. "Isn't it?" he returned fiercely.

"You were only a kid yourself," she countered.

Joe kept his back to her and spoke in ragged tones. "Yes, but I knew...I could see, even if my father couldn't—" He broke off abruptly and lowered his head.

For the second time that evening, Emma was fighting back tears. "What about your dad?" she asked around the gathering knot of empathetic emotion in her throat. She remembered Joe's father as tall and stern, always arguing with Joe, or worse, withdrawing into himself. Oh, Joe, Sr., had done all the expected things, but he hadn't done them with good cheer or wit. He hadn't celebrated when Joe won his wrestling matches and eventually went on to compete in the state championships, or got into the academy. And yet Emma knew his father must have been proud.

Joe swung around to face her, his expression grim. "He never would accept his part in it, never accepted the fact that if he'd cared just enough to lay down the law to Mary and stop her from being so self-destructive that she never would have been there that night."

Emma studied the tortured light in Joe's golden brown eyes. She hadn't expected to have this conversation with him—ever—but she was glad they were having it. It explained so much. "Is that why you and your father used to fight so bitterly?"

Joe nodded. "It was always there, between us, till the day Dad died." He let out a wavering breath. "I wish...I wish now we hadn't let it end that way, but with both of us feeling the way we did—me wanting him to take responsibility for his actions, Dad refusing to ever do so, no matter what...." Joe sighed his frustration and his pain.

"He knew you loved him, Joe," Emma said, knowing how badly Joe needed to forgive his father, even if Joe himself didn't.

"Did he?"

Joe's eyes were liquid pools of gold. Emma knew in that instant how much the rift with his father had hurt him in the past and was still hurting him. Not stopping to think, only knowing what she had to do, she took him into her arms and held him close. "Yes," she said softly, her head resting against the solidness of his shoulder, "he did, Joe. He just wasn't a very demonstrative man."

"Neither was your father," Joe said sympathetically.

Emma drew back to look into his face. "Maybe that's why we needed each other so urgently back then," she said quietly.

"Maybe," Joe agreed, but the rapacious light in his eyes reminded her that mutual consolation wasn't all that was involved in their embraces.

Knowing this had gone far enough, Emma stepped back and let her hands fall awkwardly to her sides.

"I'm sorry I didn't tell you about this first," Joe said. He shook his head bewilderedly. "I didn't even mean to tell Bobby."

"I know. You don't talk about your pain."

"And yet somehow you understand, anyway," Joe marveled aloud.

"People make mistakes, Joe," Emma countered, knowing she had made her fair share of them, too. "We all have regrets, Joe, all of us. The trick is not to let them rule your life."

He shoved both his hands through his hair, for an instant looking more the sweet boy she had loved than the strong individualist he had grown into. "I wish it were that simple for me, Emma."

"But it's not."

"No." Again, the depth of Joe's hurt surfaced as he paced back and forth and explained in a low, tortured voice, "I think my dad did what was easiest for him at the time, not what he knew in his heart was best. His lack of courage in dealing with Mary cost us our relationship and my sister her life. And for that," Joe finished heavily, his mind made up, "I just can't forgive him."

Chapter Seven

Joe intercepted Emma as she headed for her car the following morning, briefcase in hand. "Got time for a cup of coffee?" he asked casually.

Was there a problem with his house? He hadn't changed his mind about listing it, had he? "Sure," Emma said, their intimate conversation of the night before still fresh in her mind. "If we make it a quick one, that is," she amended, trying not to notice how good-natured and wide awake he looked so early in the morning. "I've got an appointment to show a house at ten, so I've got to be at the office by nine-thirty."

"No problem," Joe dismissed her concerns confidently, leading her into his house. "The coffee's already brewed and I even have a coffee cake from the bakery."

Emma followed him inside, still wondering what this was about, but the second they were in the living room, she knew.

"Oh, Joe," she gasped in pleasure as she looked around at the finished walls and gleaming white baseboard. The old carpet had been ripped up and hauled off. What upholstered furniture was left had been slipcovered in plain navy and burgundy and jewel green. The solid wood pieces had been cleaned up and polished to a soft sheen. "It's lovely."

Joe looked with satisfaction at the newly slip-covered furniture and even the unfinished wood floor. "Makes all the difference, doesn't it?" he surmised, as impressed as she was with the transformation his home had undergone in such a short time. "And wait until you see the kitchen." A hand to her spine, he guided her into the sunlit room.

"The wallpaper!" Emma said, surprised. It was a warm country print of navy, burgundy, emerald green and beige.

"You like it?" he asked, worried she wouldn't.

"Like it!" Emma exclaimed, having wondered what pattern Joe had finally decided upon among the seven possibles they had picked out together. "It's wonderful." She put down her briefcase and purse and twirled around. "The prospective buyers are going to fall in love with this kitchen."

"It'll look even better when we get the new tile in."

"And the carpet," Emma agreed, breathing in deeply of the coffee-scented air. "When are they coming out?"

"Tomorrow morning, first thing." Joe got down two mugs from the cabinets and filled them with the fragrant black brew. "Cream and sugar?"

"Black, please." She accepted the steaming mug from his hands and seated herself in a chair at the ta-ble. Even though she had been there several times before over the course of the past ten days, the room seemed suddenly small and intimate.

"So how's Bobby feeling this morning?" Joe asked, concerned.

A sigh of resignation whispered through Emma. In retrospect, she felt like such a fool for having called Joe over like that. Especially since it hadn't even occurred to her to ask her only son what he'd had to eat prior to the onset of his stomachache. "A lot better than last night," she said in answer to Joe's question, moving the coffee cup to her lips and trying not to notice how his golden brown gaze focused ever so discreetly on the movement. "The indigestion's gone, anyway," she continued.

"But?" Joe prodded, sensing there was more.

Emma put down her cup slowly. "I think he's embarrassed that we know not just what he did, but how desperate he is to fit in."

"He's had a tough time of it, hasn't he?" Joe asked sympathetically, readily seeing her worry.

"Yes, he has," Emma said softly. She looked deep into Joe's eyes and knew she could tell him anything and he would understand, even though he'd never gone through it himself. Her chilled fingers cupping the warmth of her mug, she continued unhappily, "Unfortunately, it gets worse. We had a heart-to-heart talk this morning over breakfast. He told me he had flunked algebra deliberately because he doesn't want to go on to high school next year."

"Why not?" Joe echoed, looking as confused as Emma felt.

She had never felt more a failure as a mother than she did at that moment. "He's afraid he'll be even more of an outcast there than he is at the junior high. I'm really worried about him, Joe," she confessed in a low, distressed tone. She hadn't meant to get into all this with him, but once she had started there seemed to be no stopping.

"I don't want him being that unhappy," she finished thickly, and to her horror, tears started in her eyes. Embarrassed color flooding her cheeks, she reached into her handbag and found a Kleenex.

"Hey," Joe soothed, reaching forward to touch her shoulder reassuringly, "it's going to be okay."

Emma nodded. She wanted nothing more at that moment than to lose herself in Joe's arms, to know again the comfort he was capable of giving. But she couldn't do that for so many reasons. There was still so much Joe didn't know, so much she sensed he would be unable to forgive her and Skip for. All she had to do was remember the years and years he'd held a grudge against his father...

"Bobby's a bright, resourceful kid," Joe continued his pep talk matter-of-factly.

Emma mopped up the tears on her cheeks. "I know. But his being bright doesn't mean he can cope any better with all the problems teenagers face growing up these days." She shook her head in consternation. "I don't know, Joe. We thought we were doing the right thing, letting him skip those two grades. But now... he's right, he is so much smaller than everyone else in his grade, so much younger. Because of that, he hasn't had much opportunity to play sports.

All his friends will have their drivers' licenses ahead of him. Who's he going to ask to the prom?"

"Whoa." Joe pushed aside their coffee mugs and took both her hands in his callused palms. "The situation is not nearly as hopeless as you're painting it, Emma." His fingers tightened over hers, sending out streamers of warmth and concern. "Bobby just needs to be more involved in the social aspects of life."

"You think so?" She knew he was right, but she needed to hear him say it, needed to see it in his eyes.

"Yes, I do," Joe said firmly, making no move to release the warm grasp he held on her hands. "It's just as important for him to grow that way as it is for him to grow intellectually." He paused as the next inspiration hit, then offered enthusiastically, "I'll tell you what. Why don't you let me take Bobby with me this evening for some male bonding? We could go down to the pool hall, shoot a few games."

Emma remembered Joe doing the same for Skip, how he had helped him fit in with the other guys, be less of a nerd. It was odd how history repeated itself, odd that Joe would be the one helping out Bobby after all that had happened, after all the bad feelings. But maybe that, too, would be put behind them now.

She studied Joe. For someone who, less than a week ago, had been determined to keep her at arm's length, he was awfully eager to get involved with her and her son. And with Skip, too, in an offhand sort of way. Although part of her wanted that, another part of her, the more sensible part, was wary of the risk.

The closer he got to her, the more she wanted to confide in him. Not about the past—she knew he'd never forgive her if he had even the slightest idea how she and Skip had betrayed him—but about the present, their everyday lives. Unfortunately, there was a grave risk in that, too, because Emma had to constantly censor herself when she talked to Joe. She had to remind herself what he knew and what he didn't. She had to protect Bobby, too. And she had to honor her promise to Skip...

Mistaking the reason behind her indecision, Joe teased, "It's just a pool hall, Emma. Not a den of iniquity."

She grinned back at him. *It's just one night, Emma,* she told herself reassuringly. *And it would help Bobby so much.* "You wouldn't mind?" she asked cautiously, wishing all the while that this were easier, that she and Skip both didn't have so much to hide from Joe.

"I'd enjoy it," Joe reassured her kindly. "Besides," he continued as he pushed his chair back and got up to pour them both some more coffee. "It'd give me an excuse to get out of this house. All the redecorating, twenty-four hours a day—it's kind of getting to me, if you know what I mean."

Emma grinned, sensing that was an understatement and a half on Joe's part. "I do," she said sympathetically, adding, "everybody needs a break. And—" she consulted her watch and found far too much time had passed, but then it always did when she was with Joe "—speaking of breaks, mine's about over. I've got to get to the office."

Joe accepted her leave-taking graciously and didn't try to delay it. "I'll walk you out."

"Thanks for the coffee," she said, reclaiming both her handbag and her briefcase.

"Anytime." Joe held the door for her. Emma was forced to brush by him, forced to inhale another whiff of his subtle sandalwood-and-spice cologne. Telling herself that was definitely not a thrill spiraling downward into her middle, she stepped briskly down the steps and onto the sidewalk.

Joe kept pace with her easily, taking one and a half steps for her every two. Shoving his hands in the pockets of his jeans, he asked, "What time should I stop by for Bobby?"

Emma calculated the time he would need to eat dinner and do his homework, then said, "Seven. And Joe?" She paused, trying to be tactful. "It'll have to be an early night. He's got school tomorrow."

Joe grinned. "I get the message, Em. I won't corrupt him."

Emma knew that. It was herself she was hoping he'd corrupt.

"YOU MEAN I get to go play pool with Joe, just me and him? Cool!" Bobby said when Emma affirmed this was so.

"Just be sure you have your homework done before then," Emma said.

"No problem," Bobby said, looking more animated and happy than he had in weeks.

And, Emma was pleased to discover, her son was as good as his word. By six-forty-five he was sitting by the front door, hair combed so carefully that even his cowlick had stayed down, his shirt buttoned up to the top and neatly tucked in. Too late, Emma realized it would've been better for Bobby had he left his hair messy and put on an old Bears T-shirt or something, but not knowing how to tell her son that without ripping his confidence to shreds, she kept silent. And again, to her relief, Joe saved the day.

He rang the doorbell promptly at seven o'clock and Bobby ran to get it. "Mom, look!" Bobby said excitedly, dragging a sheepish looking Joe in to show her. "Joe's got his Desert Storm hat on and a real Navy sweatshirt."

Joe did look fine, Emma couldn't help but note. The jeans were new and dark blue and not at all tight, and yet they still managed to outline the sensual lines of his well-honed body, from the muscular calves and long brawny thighs to the flat plain of his abdomen and the well-endowed apex of his thighs. He'd pulled his bill cap low over his brow but the brim did nothing to hide the slightly mischievous lights in his golden brown eyes. His jaw sporting the beginnings of a five o'clock shadow, which served to remind Emma that real men didn't dress up for a night out with the "guys." In fact, in direct contrast to Bobby's buttoned-up, slicked-down appearance, the more rumpled they looked, the better.

"It's a little nippy out there tonight," Joe said, handing Bobby a dark blue sweatshirt and a hat, both emblazoned with the words Desert Storm. Both were well broken in. "Thought you might like to have these. Since you're so into the Navy."

Bobby stared at the treasures in his hand, so thrilled that he was literally speechless. If only it had been as easy to make Emma that happy years ago, he mused. They might be married now. Bobby might be his son, instead of Skip's. But it hadn't worked out, he reminded himself, because Emma hadn't supported him in his choice of career. And for all he knew, she still didn't.

Bobby stared back up at Joe, his blue eyes huge as he cradled the Navy gear in his hands like the most precious of treasures. "I'm borrowing them, right, just for tonight?" Bobby ascertained warily, still sounding a little awed.

"Or you can keep them," Joe said offhandedly, feeling almost embarrassed because it was so easy to impress Emma's son. "If you have any use for them."

Bobby's mouth gaped open in delight. "You mean it?" he choked out finally, bobbing up and down like a float on the surface of rippling water.

Joe grinned back fondly and clapped a hand on Bobby's shoulder. "Sure I mean it," he reassured her son gruffly. Out of his peripheral vision, he was aware of Emma watching them. As usual, when Bobby was around, she looked both pleased and wary.

Inclining his head in the direction of Bobby's bedroom, Joe said, "Go try them on and see what you think."

"Cool! Thanks, Joe. I will." Bobby dashed off to do as directed.

Watching Joe interact with her son, Emma couldn't help but think what a good father Joe would be, as well as lament that it hadn't happened for the two of them the way they had always planned. He was so gentle and kind and good, his career-minded attitude aside. "That was really nice of you," she said.

Joe shrugged and looked vaguely uncomfortable again, as if it bothered him to be alone with her even for so short a time, maybe because it reminded them both of their near-kiss Sunday evening. They both knew they would have embraced passionately if they hadn't been so fortuitously interrupted.

"I wasn't sure he had anything that would fit pool hall attire," Joe said gruffly.

Emma sighed, abruptly aware how true that was, and regretting it for her son's sake. "He really doesn't have a thing that…well, macho," she admitted softly, wishing Joe didn't see so much about her, about her son. She wanted to feel like the perfect mother in his eyes, not someone who was just doing a passable job.

Bobby was back. Gone was the button-up oxford cloth shirt. In its place, over a plain white T-shirt, was a Navy sweatshirt that fell well past his hips, and gaped at the neck. His ash blond hair had lost that just-combed look and was sticking up a little all over. But it was his smile that really caught Emma's attention. Bobby was grinning from ear to ear, looking as if he had never in his life been more delighted. He held up his hands and spun around like a break dancer on the street. "Well, Mom, how do I look?"

Like a man's man, Emma thought, like a miniature version of Joe. As she and Joe traded introspective glances, it was all she could do to blink back the tears. What would it have been like had Bobby been reared as Joe's son, instead of Skip's?

Guiltily, she tore her glance from Joe's and pushed the idea away. Wishing and fantasizing her life were different would only hurt them all. Determined not to let Joe see her thoughts, Emma stiffened her spine and said with forced cheer, "You two better be going."

Joe winked at her as he passed, then promised playfully, his expression deadpan, "We'll try to be good."

Going along with him, Emma harrumphed, then gave Joe a mock-severe glance. "Joe O'Reilly, I'm counting on you *not* to lead that son of mine astray."

Joe saluted her and, lifting Bobby's hand to his brow, helped Bobby salute her, too. In that one instant, he looked all Navy bad-boy, the kind of man who could simultaneously break her heart and show her the time of her life.

"We're counting on us, too," he teased.

"BOBBY TELLS ME he and Joe went to the pool hall last night," Skip said, his expression displeased, the next day at noon.

Her heartbeat picking up, Emma nodded. Sensing this was a conversation that needed to be held in private, she led him into the deserted coffee room. Because most of the other agents were out to lunch or showing houses and or closing deals, it was blessedly empty. "When did you two talk?"

"This morning." Too keyed up to sit on one of the upholstered sofas, Skip paced back and forth. "I called the house when you were in the shower and Bobby told me all about it." His gray eyes narrowed. "He also told me about the jalapeño peppers." Skip paused, and then went on, the hurt and the anger evident in his low tone, "Why didn't you call me, Emma?"

Emma tore her eyes from the nick on Skip's chin where he'd cut himself shaving. "I did call you, but you weren't home. And I was frantic."

"So you called Joe?" Skip prodded incredulously.

Emma lifted her stormy eyes to his. He was trying to make her feel guilty, when she had done nothing except care for Bobby's health the best way she knew how at the time. "As I said," she repeated coolly, "I was frantic. I knew Joe was home. Fortunately, no sooner had Joe gotten here than Bobby fessed up to what was really wrong. Our family doctor called back and, once he was apprised of the situation, told me what to do. Once Bobby had responded to the antacid, there was no need to call you and upset you, at least not then." Not when Joe was telling her about one of the most private and difficult times of his life.

"I think there was a need, Emma," Skip countered sternly, stepping nearer, so the two of them were almost toe to toe. "Or are you trying to cut me out of your life, to make room for Joe again?"

Emma sucked in her breath, the ferocity of Skip's attack catching her off guard. "It wasn't like that, Skip. Don't you understand? I panicked. I would have called whoever was next door."

"Oh, really? Then why not your other neighbors? Neighbors who have lived there just as long?"

Silence fell between them. Emma said nothing because there was nothing to say. She didn't know why she had called Joe exactly . . . or did she?

"I don't want Bobby to become a pawn between the three of us," Skip said harshly, giving her no chance to explain further.

"I don't, either," Emma admitted wearily.

"But I do want to spend more time with him." Skip paused, gauging her reaction to that. Finding it positive, he continued, "There's a Cubs game tonight. I know tomorrow is a school day, but we could see the first half or so of the game and be home by eleven."

Emma knew Bobby needed some time with his dad more than he needed his sleep. Plus it would make them both feel better. "I think that would be great," she said enthusiastically. "And Skip? I'm sorry I didn't call you sooner," she said contritely. "I was going to, but things have been so hectic that I just haven't had much of a chance."

Again, Skip was judgmentally silent. He seemed to be thinking that prior to Joe's reappearance in their lives, Emma hadn't had any difficulty finding time to call him and talk about Bobby, no matter how busy she was. And he was right.

Chastened, she realized she would have to be careful not to lean on Joe in ways she had previously leaned on Skip, just because of his physical proximity.

Skip steered the conversation back to their plans. "Then I can pick him up after school?" he asked.

Emma nodded, relieved Skip would be spending time with Bobby, too. Because right now, Bobby needed all the male bonding he could get. "Thanks, Skip," she said.

But once again, it seemed, inadvertently, she had done the wrong thing. "You don't have to thank me, Emma," Skip said stiffly, his aggravation mounting once again. "He's my son. I love him. I'm only doing what any good father would."

SKIP'S WORDS were still ringing in her ears when she arrived home at five-thirty. Joe was busy mowing his yard, the suntanned muscles of his bare back gleaming in the warm May sun. Seeing her, he lifted a hand in greeting and went on. Tearing her eyes from his masculine form with effort—he was so handsome and graceful and undeniably male that she had the feeling she could stand there and watch him cut the grass all day—Emma retrieved the mail and went on into the house.

Just because Bobby was off with Skip, there was no reason for her to feel so lonely, she told herself firmly. Bobby spent at least half of every week with Skip and had for years. Normally, she welcomed the quiet time to herself. But that had been before Joe came back into her life. Now she was lonely and restless and edgy, full of energy she just couldn't expend no matter how hard she worked.

But she was going to have to try, Emma decided deliberately as she shucked her office clothes and traded them in for knee-length khaki shorts and a white knit shirt. Perhaps a little housecleaning was in order.

She was just getting out the mop and the bucket when the doorbell rang. As she glanced through the viewer, she saw Joe standing on her front porch, his dark brow furrowed in perplexity. His features relaxed the moment she opened the front door and smiled at him through the screen. "You know a lot about flowers, don't you?" he asked without preamble, crushing Emma's hopes that he'd come for something other than house-selling-related advice.

"I know *some,*" Emma qualified, trying not to notice how the T-shirt he'd shrugged on—obviously for her benefit—clung to his sweat-damp skin, or how her own stomach fluttered at his nearness.

"Well, that's more than I know," Joe admitted, wiping his damp forehead on his sleeve.

If he was thinking about anything other than business, Emma thought wryly, it would be hard to tell. In sharp contrast to her own overly aroused mood, he looked as if he couldn't be less physically aware of her. Not that she should be disappointed. Relieved, rather. But she wasn't relieved, Emma admitted, which just went to show what a closet romantic she was.

"Listen," Joe said impatiently, blissfully unaware of the licentious nature of her thoughts, "would you mind taking a look at this foliage at the rear of my property? I'm having a heck of a time trying to figure out what's a weed and what's a flower."

It was a neighborly request, that was all, and considering the state of his property, not an unexpected one. "Sure," Emma said just as casually, trying not to feel disappointed he hadn't come over on a more personal errand, or even just to talk or because he wanted to see her. Nevertheless, as she recalled how he'd looked just minutes before, shirtless, the bare work-chiseled muscles of his chest and back gleaming golden in the late afternoon sunshine, her heartbeat picked up in anticipation of being close to him again. "Just let me get my shoes," she said.

She found her socks and sneakers and put them on. Together they walked to the back of his property. "You did a nice job with the lawn," Emma remarked, noting without wanting to the flush of sun across his cheeks, and the shallowness of her own breaths.

Joe accepted her compliment with a shrug. To Emma's growing disappointment, he continued to look completely unaware of her except on the most cursory platonic level. "I've always liked cutting grass," he admitted.

And she had always enjoyed watching him cut it, Emma reflected wryly, telling herself that once again she was acting like an oversexed teenager. From the time he had moved in next door, Emma had always liked watching him push the mower around. Although back then he hadn't had the powerful build he had now. Then, he'd been a boy. Now, it was clearer than ever Joe was a man.

Abruptly, Emma realized what she was doing—again—and pushed the erotic thoughts of Joe away. Forcing herself to concentrate only on the foliage she'd been brought to identify, Emma glanced in the direction Joe gestured. Suddenly, his urgent need of her was clear. Just looking at the mess he was trying to untangle gave Emma pause.

Years ago, the thick foliage in front of the chain-link fence that enclosed Joe's backyard had been a neatly landscaped bed of flowers and shrubs. In the past couple of years, however, it had become a jungle of intertwined leafy green plants.

"See?" Joe pointed to a thin branch with small green leaves. "I think this is a forsythia bush."

Being careful not to brush up against him, Emma leaned in to examine the branch. "You're right about that. I remember seeing the yellow flowers earlier in the month." The forsythia bushes had originally formed a neat hedge along the rear of the property. In the ten years since Joe had gone to the academy, however, they had not been trimmed, and had grown out and over the other flowering bushes, totally engulfing them. As Emma looked at the foliage she was reminded of the tangle of extra threads at the bottom of her sewing basket. Part of her said it wasn't worth the work of trying to untangle the mess. But the other part of her, the devoted weekend gardener, told her it would be a crime not to try to save the bushes that had already endured so many harsh Illinois winters.

Emma pointed to a prickly sticker bush three feet high. "This is a weed."

"I know that," Joe said, looking at her in mock exasperation.

Her heart turning cartwheels in her chest at the sudden, boyish playfulness of his mood, Emma grinned back at Joe. "I figured as much," she retorted dryly. Her mood lifting buoyantly, she picked up a hoe that was lying on the ground and chopped the offending weed neatly at the root, then used the toe of her sneaker to kick it aside.

"Very good." Joe leaned against a garden rake and cast an appreciative look at her leg. "I could've used you earlier."

"Don't get any ideas about me doing *all* the work," she teased, finding relief from the tension she felt every time she was this physically close to him by joshing him right back. "I said I'd take a look at this mess. Not hire on for free slave labor."

Joe flashed her an easy, favor-coaxing grin. "Can't blame a guy for trying, can you?"

That all depended, Emma thought. If he meant now, no. If he meant earlier in the week, when he'd made a very deliberate pass at her...when he knew all the while how frankly incompatible their lives had become and still had almost kissed her and she had almost let him, that was something else. As drawn as she was to Joe, she didn't want to be hurt. And a temporary fling with him would hurt her. If she were to be with him again, it would be even harder for her to see him leave. And he was leaving again. By selling his house, he was cutting ties with Evanston permanently, even if he had yet to really admit that to himself.

As her look turned serious, so, abruptly, did Joe's.

Getting back down to business, he said, "It's these tall bushes in the middle that I'm most concerned about." Joe carefully grasped a long skinny branch between two fingers and pulled it out of the tangle of overgrown foliage for her to see. "See the thorns here?"

Emma nodded. The branch was covered with them.

"Do you think these could be rosebushes?"

It looked like it, but she didn't want to make any promises until she had inspected the whole plant or plants and was sure what they were dealing with. "To tell you much of anything, Joe, I'll really need to see the base of the plants, near the roots."

Joe frowned. Carefully, he transferred the thorny branch to her, then with his free hand, held the heavy branches of the forsythia aside. Emma knelt beside him, aware they were touching now from thigh to shoulder, and that there was no helping it, any more than she could help the reflexive pounding of her heart or the shallowness of her breath. Forcing herself to focus only on the bushes and not on Joe, she flattened a bunch of weeds and scrunched down lower for a better look. "Yep, those are rosebushes, all right. Climbing roses to the rear, and shrub roses in front of those. Azaleas in front of those. But they're sadly neglected, Joe. I don't see a bloom on any of them."

Finished with their inspection, Joe leaned back on his heels, as did she, and gently let the bushes go. He looked over at her, his golden brown eyes full of hope. "Think we could get them flowering again?" he asked.

He was talking about a tremendous amount of work, Emma thought. But work held salvation. Because it would save them, her especially, from thoughts of what might have been. "We could probably get them flowering again, with a lot of tender loving care," she allowed cautiously, "but first we'll have to untangle everything and cut back all of the forsythia bushes to a manageable size."

Joe grinned and lounged lazily back on the newly mown grass. In no hurry to get to work, he picked up a shorn blade, tossed it at her nose and laughed when she batted it away and threw one right back. "I noticed a 'we' in there." Joe's glance roved her from head to toe before settling firmly on her eyes. "Does that mean you're willing to help?"

She liked it when he was like this, easygoing and flirtatious, Emma realized, but then she always had. That had been most of the problem. Even at seventeen, she'd known she found him far too attractive for her own good. "I guess I just volunteered, didn't I?" she retorted, amazed at her willingness to be so close to him, despite all the hurts of the past and the secrets still keeping them apart.

But the complexity of the situation didn't end there. Ever since she'd trotted out here with Joe, she had ceased to feel lonely and at loose ends anymore. In fact, lounging here next to him on the grass, she felt anything but lonely. And that was as dangerous to her as it was pleasurable.

"Now or later?" Joe asked.

"Now," Emma said. *While Skip and Bobby are otherwise occupied and I don't have to explain myself to either of them.* Or worry about how nervously or jealously Skip would react to the idea of her spending so much time one on one with Joe. She knew that it was a risk she just shouldn't be taking.

"Great." Joe leaped to his feet. "Hang on," he said. "I'll get some shears from the garage. And extra gloves, too."

He was back minutes later and, toiling side by side like a well-rehearsed team, the two of them went to work. Fortunately for Emma's already overheated sensibilities, the chore took all her powers of concentration. Branches of all four types of shrubs were braided together. Talking only about who should hold or cut what, Emma separated them, and Joe snipped where she directed. One hour passed and then another. Slowly but surely, the landscaped area that ran the entire width of his backyard began to take shape.

Emma was satisfied with the way their task was progressing, but as for Joe, it was hard to tell what he was thinking. He was all business as they worked. Civil but remote. So much so that Emma began to get a little nervous, to wonder if maybe he had somehow begun to suspect what she'd done years ago. And that was when it happened. A particularly thick and springy three-tiered branch of a climbing rosebush slipped from Emma's fingers and lashed Joe across the back. He sucked in his breath and swore vividly. It was easy to see why. The thorns had cut right through the fabric of his T-shirt and into his skin. When he jerked forward to get away from the punishing lash, the branch moved right along with him, digging in further and inflicting even greater pain.

"Oh, Joe," Emma breathed, all the color draining from her face as she rushed forward to extricate the thorny branch from his back. "I'm so sorry."

Joe gritted his teeth. "No problem," he said, though sweat had beaded on his forehead and blood was staining his shirt in three perpendicular slashes from shoulder blade to midspine.

"Let me help you," Emma said, already reaching for the hem of his T-shirt.

To her exasperation, Joe shook his head. "No," he said curtly, recoiling from her touch. "I can handle it."

Looking at the whiteness of his face, Emma wasn't so sure of that. She knew only that he didn't want her touching him in so intimate a way, and that saddened and disappointed her. "But how will you reach the cuts?" she protested quietly, still feeling so very guilty for having been the cause of his injury.

Joe clenched his teeth; she could tell from the pained look on his face that he was trying not to wince. "I'll just go stand under the shower," he said, enunciating each word through short, shallow breaths. "I'm pretty grimy from working in the yard all day, anyway."

Still feeling guilty as hell, Emma looked back at the bushes. "I'll finish up here,' she promised quietly.

"No." Joe's refusal was curt and swift. "I don't want you getting cut, too."

She stepped back quickly, trying but failing to hide her hurt.

"I think you should go home. Really, Emma." His voice softened unexpectedly and he touched her shoulder gently, the implacable harshness in his attitude fading as quickly as it had appeared. "I can finish this up in the morning. You've done more than enough."

As she looked up at him, Emma could tell Joe really had appreciated her help. And that he had never been more anxious in his life to get rid of her.

YOU HANDLED THAT ONE like a pro, Joe told himself as he shed his grimy clothes and stepped into the shower. He'd made Emma feel like a real jerk when all she'd done was help him all evening. And why?

Because too late he had realized working with her in the yard was not such a hot idea. Every time she had bent or knelt or reached, his eyes had been drawn to the long supple lines of her hips and thighs beneath her snug-fitting khaki shorts and the roundness of her breasts beneath the clinging white cotton shirt. Long sleeved and knit, the shirt had a row of tiny close-set buttons that ran from the provocative line of her collarbone to an inch below her breasts. She'd left the top two buttons undone and the skin he had glimpsed there beneath the open flap had been as smooth and golden and silky looking as ever.

He had wanted to kiss her so badly.

Hell, why not be honest, Joe thought as he soaped himself furiously. He had wanted to haul her into his arms and kiss her until her knees were weak and she was limp and warm and cuddly against him, until she looked at him with eyes that were dark with desire and lips that were wet and soft and open with longing. He had wanted to hold her and touch her until she had told him that what had happened years ago had been the biggest mistake of her life, until she told him she wanted him still, until she told him that there was a future for them yet.

But it hadn't happened. And it wasn't likely to, either, he informed himself grimly.

No, she had a home here, a career. Even if she wanted to get involved with him again—and she'd made it clear that she didn't by the way she practically jumped every time he got anywhere near to touching her—nothing would ever come of it.

And even if by some miracle of fate, it did . . .

He sensed leaving her this time would be a hell of a lot harder than leaving her had been a decade before. Because now he knew what he hadn't then: that there was no other woman for him on this earth, that there was no substitute for Emma. . . .

Chapter Eight

Emma had just gotten out of the tub and pulled on the thick white terry-cloth robe Bobby and Skip had given her for Mother's Day when the doorbell rang. Belting the calf-length garment tightly around her, she padded barefoot to the door. A glance through the viewer revealed Joe standing on the other side of the door. His dark hair had been washed and blown dry. He had on knee-length shorts, socks and shoes, but his shirt was in his hand.

Knowing something must be wrong—otherwise he would've been completely dressed—she opened the door, and asked, not bothering to mask her concern, "How's your back?"

Joe grimaced. "Would you believe still bleeding? And I don't have a Band-Aid in the house. I don't suppose you have any," he finished hopefully.

Emma opened the screen door and ushered him inside. "I've also got antiseptic," she added helpfully.

He dismissed her offer with a terse shake of his head. "You don't have to bother with that."

"The hell I don't, Joe O'Reilly!" Emma retorted as her deeply ingrained nurturing instinct took over. "You're not getting an infected back on my account."

He looked at her robe. His golden brown glance narrowed, and he seemed suddenly uncomfortable as he asked, "Is this a bad time?"

Whether it was or not was immaterial now. Emma figured it was too late to be modest. Besides, the robe had the luxurious thickness of three layers of toweling, so it wasn't as if Joe could see anything except a tightly belted garment that almost covered her from head to foot.

"Nope. I had finished my bubble bath." Aware of the intentness of his gaze—had he guessed she was naked save for a pair of panties beneath the robe?— she led the way. "Come on in the kitchen and have a seat on the stool. I'll get the first-aid kit."

Joe watched as she returned. Self-consciously, Emma opened up the kit. "This must hurt," she murmured as she looked at the gashes, feeling guilty all over again.

"It's not so bad now," Joe said, seeming relieved she was there to minister to him despite the exasperation she heard in his voice. Clearly, it embarrassed him to have to come to her for help. "It's annoying as hell, of course. If it would just stop bleeding . . ."

"It will, once we get the antiseptic and bandages on," Emma reassured him. Acutely aware of the warmth and the smoothness of his skin, she dabbed each of the three long scrapes with antiseptic then used the tip of her index finger to smooth on antibiotic cream. Joe was so still that he seemed almost not to breathe, yet she could feel the increasing rigidity in the muscles of his shoulders and back as she progressed from the first scrape to the second to the third. "Am I hurting you?" she asked softly.

Wordlessly, he shook his head. He was silent a moment, then sighed harshly. "Although I'd understand if maybe you wanted to hurt me," Joe muttered, more to himself than to her.

Stunned, Emma finished what she was doing and moved around so she could see his face.

"I've had a lot of time to think the past ten days, while I've been cleaning up and painting and working out in the yard," Joe said quietly. He regarded her gravely. "I know I hurt you when I left, and I'm sorry about that, Emma." He swallowed hard. "You can't know how much."

Emma ducked her head as she felt helpless tears spring to her eyes. For days after Joe had left her, she had dreamed of his saying this to her. But now it was too late. They couldn't go back and pretend nothing had ever happened, even if they wanted to, because so much *had* happened. And Joe wouldn't forgive her if he knew what she had done. And she didn't see how she could be intimate with him again and not tell him, even though everything in her was straining toward just such a reconciliation.

She stepped back a pace, her knees shaking beneath the robe. She'd never felt more vulnerable and exposed than she did right now. "Band-Aids aren't going to work on that back of yours," she said, telling herself firmly to forget about the past and concentrate instead on caring for his scrapes. "I've got some gauze in the bathroom. I'll get it."

JOE WATCHED her leave, his heart heavy with disappointment. So she wasn't going to forgive him for putting the Navy ahead of her. What had he expected? That the years would have changed her feelings about that, too? He knew he needed a woman who would be not only supportive of his career, but able to cope during his long absences, when he was at sea. Emma was independent now, certainly, but as for her supporting his career, that seemed as unlikely as ever. Not once since he had been back had she asked him about his work. That alone spoke volumes.

Emma returned, sterile gauze in hand. She handed him a dispenser of clear surgical tape and then began unrolling the gauze. When she had a strip approximately twelve inches long, she cut it off.

He sat silently as she bandaged first one scrape, and then the next, and the next. Her hands moved over him coolly and efficiently. He felt her breath on his neck and breathed in the scent of her. She smelled good, Joe thought. Damn good. Like a bouquet of wildflowers. And woman. Mature, sensual woman.

And she looked good, too, he thought, watching as she capped the antiseptic and antibiotic and put the unused Band-Aids away. She'd twisted her honey blond hair and pinned it up for her bath. Tendrils escaped down her neck, sideswept bangs framed her face. She wore no makeup. She looked younger without it, more vulnerable. More like the Emma he used to know.

"Stop it," she said in a quavering voice, closing the top of her red-and-white first-aid kit with a snap.

Joe's head lifted. Belatedly, he realized he was still clutching his clean shirt in his hand. He wasn't sure if she'd said anything else to him because he hadn't been listening. He'd been intent only on drinking her in. Marveling at her nearness. Her sheer womanliness. He struggled to pull his attention back to the conversation at hand. "Stop what?" he asked huskily.

She took a deep ragged breath, looking as if she might burst into tears at any moment. "Stop looking at me like that," she ordered, her lip trembling. "Like you want to devour me here and now, because it's not going to happen. Do you hear me, Joe? It's not going to happen!"

She started to brush past him, to cut him out of her life once again. Suddenly it was all too much for Joe— the pretending they no longer cared about each other, pretending they no longer loved each other or wanted each other. She did want him, he could see that yearning beneath the raw anger and pent-up emotion and vulnerability on her face.

If nothing else, by God, they would be honest with each other, he vowed. He caught her by the waist and pulled her between his legs. He'd been hard almost as long as he'd been in the house. And from the way she was trembling, he was willing to bet she was aching, too.

"Then you stop looking at me, too," he said, pushing aside his doubts about her and concentrating only on what he was feeling. His voice dropped a husky, caressing notch as he wove his hands through her hair and tilted her face up so it was just beneath his. "Stop looking at me like you want to tell me something, but won't. Or can't. Stop looking at me like you're mentally taking me to bed. Stop reminding me in a hundred different ways that we once meant *everything* to each other."

Emma swayed on her feet, the edge of her hips bumping against his inner thigh. "I'm not—" she denied, but she couldn't quite meet his eyes as she spoke.

Joe let his hands down her arms. "The hell you're not," he said, as his palms slid over her forearms, then dropped away from her altogether. "You could have changed out of this robe the minute you let me in this house. You didn't."

Her face flushing a fiery pink, Emma started to step back. "I didn't see any reason—"

"Or maybe you had a reason," he said, all the anger and frustration he'd felt these long years and weeks and days coming to the fore as he anchored both hands around her waist once again. "Maybe you wanted to seduce me."

"No—" Breathless, she tried to twist free; he wasn't about to let her. Not when they were finally being honest with each other. Or as honest as she would let them be.

"Okay, then," Joe said, tossing out another possibility as he continued to watch her uptilted face, "maybe you want me to seduce you." At his words, Emma was silent, trembling. So much so that he knew he was right. "Maybe you don't want to be responsible for what's going to happen," Joe continued.

"I've always been responsible!" Emma cried, shoving at his chest with surprising force. "Even when you haven't."

Stunned by the pent-up fury he heard in her voice, Joe let her go. He stared at the tears he saw gathering in her bright blue eyes. "What's that supposed to mean?" he demanded impatiently.

She turned away from him so he couldn't see her face. "Nothing," she replied in a flat, dull voice.

Taken aback by her unexpected flare-up, he continued to watch her, "Emma—"

"It was nothing, I said." She whirled toward him, her expression stony. "Now get out," she ordered, clamping both hands at her waist. Probably because of the stunned look on his face, she amended in a softer, more reasonable voice, "Please. I'd like to get dressed."

He regarded her silently. She was doing it again, hitting him with secrets, lies and evasions. Joe's mouth tightened. He rose, every inch of him hard and aching . . . and disappointed. It wasn't going to happen. She wasn't going to be here waiting for him, not now, not ever. "With pleasure," he said tightly. He turned on his heel and left.

JOE WAS RIGHT, Emma thought. A part of her did want to seduce him, and the other part of her wanted to be seduced, to just have it happen so she wouldn't have to think about right or wrong.

She sighed. It wasn't like her to be so irresponsible. So driven by her emotions. But then, that was the way she had always been around Joe. He made her realize how much she needed; he made her want. And the truth was, since he had been out of her life, all this time there had been a singular loneliness that nothing—not Skip, not her love for Bobby, not her work—could erase.

She didn't want to get back on that merry-go-round of thwarted desires. And yet . . . the bitter irony of it was, after all this time, she finally felt she had it in her to be the kind of strong, independent wife a career Navy officer like Joe needed.

She could cope now with the long months he was at sea.

But she couldn't erase the past. And that hurt more than anything.

Slowly, Emma walked back to her bedroom and began to dress. Skip would have Bobby home from the ball game in another hour, she noted as she pulled on a pair of peach slacks and a summery white sweater. She took the pins out of her hair and brushed it a hundred strokes.

Again, the doorbell rang.

Thinking it was Skip and Bobby a little early, she went to get it, and again found Joe O'Reilly on her doorstep. He was wearing a shirt this time, and he carried a big bouquet of flowers in his hand. He thrust them at her, and accepting them wordlessly, she stepped out onto the porch.

"I'm sorry," he said, his glance simple and direct. "I had no right to blow up at you like that, especially after all you've done for me."

"You were right, Joe. I should have dressed before I let you in." She ran a hand through the silky, just-brushed smoothness of her hair. "I don't know what I was thinking."

Oh, yes you do.

Joe shook his head, dismissing her apology. "I'm not some sex maniac, Emma. I'm capable of being around a woman in a robe without going all crazy."

Except with you, Joe amended silently. *What you do to me, Emma, is something else again.*

"Still—"

"Can't we just forget it?" he asked.

She lifted her face to his, glad she hadn't bothered to turn on the porch light. She liked the way the moonlight gilded the strong, masculine lines of his face. She liked the way he had come back so promptly to make peace so they wouldn't have to worry about their anger with each other all night. And she wondered at her loss of resolve where he was concerned.

"Forget what?" She grinned back.

He didn't answer; merely looked pleased. "Can I have a hug?" he asked genially, with the affection of an old, dear friend.

Wanting to make up as much as he did, Emma nodded. The next thing she knew she was in his arms, every warm male inch of him pressed up against every soft female inch of her. Immediately, she felt his arousal. She heard his sharp intake of breath, echoed by her own, and knew that this part of his apology hadn't been planned. Her heart pounding, she drew back, ever so slightly.

"Oh, Emma," he whispered as he looked down at her, and then his head lowered, their mouths met, and the memories that had made up a thousand fantasies became her reality once again. His kiss, his touch was so familiar that it felt as if they had never been apart. It felt like coming home, and never, Emma thought, had anything been so wonderful. He tasted like peppermint, he kissed like a dream—with tenderness and skill and passion. She melted against him and laced her arms about his neck. He responded by holding her just as tightly, and then all was lost in the pleasurable ongoing sensation of the kiss.

She was shaking when he let her go.

He looked as if he felt just as unsteady.

"I guess we made up." His voice was gruff when at last he spoke.

She nodded, and somehow, with a great deal of difficulty, found her voice. "I guess we did," she responded inanely.

He stepped back, looking every bit as sorry to go as she was to let him. And yet, Emma thought, they both knew it was best, that they weren't ready to let this go any further than it already had. "I guess I'll see you around, then," he said awkwardly.

"I guess you will," Emma said softly.

And as he turned and walked down her steps, she found herself hoping it was soon.

EMMA WALKED on air the whole next day. She had three back-to-back closings and an appointment schedule that normally would have made her tense, but today nothing fazed her. She was just so happy. And she knew why. It had to do with the kiss . . . and the fight . . . and the fact that they'd made up. It was all beginning to feel so normal. As if they were on their way to being lovers again. And she wanted normalcy with Joe. So very badly.

The trouble was, she just wasn't sure it would ever really be possible for them to have an enduring relationship, even long distance. Sure, things were good now, but realistically, how long could that last?

Every time he looked at Bobby or dealt with Skip, she was suffused with mingled feelings of guilt and apprehension. She wanted Joe to understand why she had married Skip when she had. She wanted him to know that she hadn't done it out of spite, as he still thought, but out of necessity because her father had left her and she'd needed a husband and a home.

It hurt her that he still thought she'd been faithless and fickle. She feared if they became lovers, he'd distrust her in the future, especially around other men or when he was away.

Still, Joe was a smart, secure man. Mature enough to realize she'd changed, that she no longer needed a man in her day-to-day life, but could function quite independently on her own. If he was willing to see her whenever and wherever they could and be content with that, she could be content, too. As for the past, there she had no choice. It would have to remain a secret and she would have to continue the lie. Skip was right; to do otherwise would risk the foundation of all their lives.

In the meantime, she'd appreciate the normalcy that had sprung up between her and Joe. She wasn't sure finding him in her garage with Bobby when she came home from work was what she meant by normalcy, however. In shorts and a tank top, his dark hair tousled, his skin tanned and glowing with health, he looked magnificent. And perfectly at ease as he assembled a barbell. "I'm giving my old weight set to Bobby," he explained. "It's just been gathering dust down in the basement."

Emma recalled seeing the set beneath the piles of clutter that had been in his basement. She had just assumed that he'd sold it with the rest of his unneeded belongings. "Why didn't you sell it in the garage sale?"

"Sentimental value, Mom," Bobby piped up knowledgeably. "Joe said he could only bear to part with this set, which he got for his fifteenth birthday, by giving it to someone very special. Me." Bobby grinned, looking even more delighted than he had when Joe had taken him out to shoot pool.

"It's okay, isn't it?" Joe asked, looking suddenly concerned. "I'll teach him how to use it and make sure he knows all the safety rules."

"It's fine," Emma finally found the wits to say. Seeing Joe, so scantily clad again, had her mind in an uproar. All she could think about was the kiss he'd given her last night. Gentle and sexy, demanding and evocative all at once, that one little kiss had kept her simmering in a state of highly charged sexual anticipation all day. And it didn't help knowing Bobby would soon be picked up by Skip—for the weekend.

"Okay, Joe, enough talking to my mom," Bobby prodded, "it's back to work."

Joe laughed at Bobby's impatience to get down to brass tacks, which was, Emma realized uncomfortably, so much like Joe's. But she couldn't, wouldn't, allow herself to think about that.

"Okay, sport," Joe continued, "now the first thing you remember is this..."

Emma left the two guys in the garage and went on into the house. The late May afternoon was warm and the house was even warmer. She had just opened the patio door and the living room windows to get some cross-ventilation going when Doris knocked on the door. Glancing up, Emma motioned her in.

Still in her Evanston Police Department uniform, Doris kicked off her shoes and joined Emma in the kitchen for a glass of lemonade. "Bobby and Joe really seem to be hitting it off."

"Yes," Emma said, wishing she could feel happier about it, "they are."

Doris studied her openly. "That bothers you," she guessed.

Knowing she could tell Doris anything and have it go no further, Emma admitted, "I just hate to see Bobby become too dependent on Joe. He'll be leaving again in another few weeks." And as much as she wanted to forget that, she knew she couldn't.

"He could still come back for visits," Doris pointed out.

Yes, he could, Emma thought. But the question was... She looked at Doris. "Will he want to?"

Doris shrugged, professing to have none of the answers. "You're the one who's been spending all the time with him. You tell me. Will he come back again?"

He would if he knew, Emma thought, then immediately pushed her guilty feelings away. The die was cast. It didn't matter what she wished she had done now. Still, it would be easier if she didn't keep having this sinking feeling she'd made a terrible mistake, one she was exacerbating by not telling him the truth now. He might forgive her—eventually—if he ever found out what she'd done then. He'd see she'd done the best she could under the circumstances when she was eighteen. But would he forgive her for keeping the truth from him now they were beginning to be close again? Or would he be angry with her for maintaining, even furthering, the lie? A chill went down her back. She knew the answer to that.

He'd feel betrayed. Horribly betrayed. Which was precisely why she couldn't tell him, Emma thought. Now that she knew he cared, she also knew how much it would hurt. Besides, she reasoned securely, maybe he didn't have to know. Especially if he was as happy as he appeared to be with things the way they were. She just had to keep reminding herself of that. In not telling Joe, she was sparing him terrible pain . . .

"Hey, Doris," Skip said, letting himself in the back door, his presence reminding Emma that it was Skip's turn to have Bobby stay with him at his house for the next few days. "How are you?"

Doris grinned at Skip. "Pretty good for a policewoman who spent half the day over at the high school, tracking down a thief who's been breaking into cars and stealing stereos. They've also been leaving behind some spray painted graffiti. Kind of a calling card. We think it might be the same group that trashed

Joe's house. Anyway, I wanted to let him know we had a lead and—"

The back door opened again. "Hi, Dad." Bobby gave Skip a welcoming hug and turned to Doris. "Joe says he can talk to you now, over at his house. We're all through."

"Music to my ears," Doris said. She looked down at the floor and her sock clad feet. "Now where'd I put my shoes?"

It didn't surprise Emma that Joe hadn't come into the kitchen with Bobby, but rather had sent him in as a messenger. Although they'd made some overtures, he and Skip still weren't that comfortable around each other.

"Your shoes are in the living room. I saw them," Bobby said.

"Got your stuff together?" Skip asked Bobby. Doris drained her glass and, after saying goodbye, made her way to the door.

"Not yet, but I'll hurry," Bobby promised. He dashed off to pack.

Emma and Skip were alone in the kitchen. "That was nice of Joe, giving Bobby his old weights," Skip said.

The nostalgic look on his face reminded Emma of something else she'd forgotten. "You and Joe both used those weights, didn't you?" she said softly.

Skip nodded, accepting the glass of lemonade Emma gave him. "Yes. It brought back a lot of memories, seeing Joe show Bobby how to bench-press." He looked down at the floor, his expression sober, repentant. "There have been times the past month I'd forgotten what good friends we once were. What good friends we all were."

Emma nodded. Skip's candid admission made it easier for her to say, "I know. I miss the camaraderie, too."

Skip looked at her in the compassionate way that reminded Emma why she had married him. Aware, as was she, that Bobby might walk in again at any minute, he chose his next words carefully. "Seeing them together . . . it makes me feel less guilty somehow. I know I've reacted selfishly of late, Emma, and I'm sorry."

"Skip, I understand," Emma was quick to assure him.

Skip sent her a skeptical glance. "Do you?" he asked in a way that let her know he expected no answer. He shook his head in obvious confusion. "Sometimes I don't know if I do," he admitted. "I just get so territorial, Emma. And that's not like me."

Skip was right, Emma thought uncomfortably, it wasn't like him. Successful, brilliant in his own right, he had no reason to be jealous of Joe. Normally, he wasn't. Only when it came to her. And Bobby. And as it stood now, he only knew the half of it. How would he react if he knew she and Joe were on their way to becoming lovers? Afraid he'd pick up on her guilt, Emma pushed the thought away. "You've been trying to protect Bobby," she soothed.

"As well as myself," Skip amended. He seemed to be wrestling with his conscience, much the same as Emma was. "I want Joe to have a positive impact on Bobby's life," he said finally.

"So do I," Emma said, troubled.

Skip's mouth thinned. "But I don't want him any closer than he is right now," he went on to stipulate firmly. He sent her an earnest look that begged for understanding. "Surely you, better than anyone, can understand that, Emma."

"Yes, I can," she said quietly. Because part of Emma felt that way, too. But another part of her felt an even deeper, very private remorse because she was now more certain than ever that she should have married Joe, not Skip, no matter how long she had to wait. They all would have been so much happier now.

Skip finished his lemonade and put his glass in the sink. "Oh, well, it won't be for much longer, anyway." He let out a weary breath. "Joe will be leaving. His house will be sold . . ."

Emma averted her glance uneasily. Skip thought that would be the end of it, but she knew better. Now that Joe had come back into their lives, nothing was ever going to be the same again. Her serenity, the equilibrium of her life, had been disturbed. Worse, as it stood now, she was not only lying to Joe, but also to Skip. He had no idea how close she and Joe were becoming, and she couldn't tell him, not yet, anyway. He would constantly fear she would want to change her mind and tell Joe the truth, and then they would all lose.

And Emma knew Skip would be right to worry. She did want to tell Joe the truth. Only her worry over how he'd react, how the news would disrupt all their lives, was stopping her.

Chapter Nine

"So first you went to the academy, where you majored in systems engineering. And then after that you went to Surface Warfare Officer School," Bobby ascertained, hanging on to Joe's every word.

Unable to remember when he'd met a kid so fascinated by his life, or one he took to so immediately, Joe smiled. "Right."

"And then you went on active duty?" Bobby continued.

"Right again."

"It sure sounds neat," Bobby lamented, looking as if he thought his own life was the dullest thing going.

Joe knew Bobby hadn't been asking thirty minutes of questions just for the sake of making conversation. "Are you interested in the academy?" he asked, wondering even as he spoke how Emma and Skip would feel about that. Would they want their son following in his footsteps?

Bobby's mouth turned down with discouragement. He rubbed the padded seat of the weight bench with the back of his hand. "The academy wouldn't take someone like me. I'm too nerdy."

"Don't sell yourself short," Joe said. "You're not nerdy. You're smart. The academy needs guys like you." He paused. "If you want, I can arrange to have a current catalog sent to you. It'll tell you all the physical and academic requirements for admission. It'd give you something to aim for. Once you're a little older, you could even go visit it in the summer."

"You mean it?" Bobby said excitedly.

Joe nodded. "I'll even take you around myself if I'm—Emma. Hi." He looked up to see her standing in the open doorway of the garage. In a trim pink jacket, white silk blouse and white skirt, a strand of pearls around her neck, she looked pretty, professional and successful. And unhappy as hell with him and Bobby. Wondering what he'd done to annoy her this time, he continued easily, "I didn't hear you come in."

Obviously, her look said.

"Bobby, what are you doing here? I thought you were going to be at your dad's today."

"I was, but Dad had a departmental meeting at four, so he said it would be okay if I came here and worked out with my new weights until dinnertime. Then he's going to pick me up. That's okay, isn't it?"

Emma nodded. "Of course." She smiled at her son. "You know we try and make this shared custody as easy as we possibly can on you."

Bobby grinned at Joe, explaining, "See, it's like I have two homes. One with Mom and one with Dad. That makes me luckier than most kids 'cause if one parent gets mad at me, I just go over to the other parent's house."

Emma sent her son a droll look that told Joe Bobby's assessment of things wasn't quite true. In fact, considering the devotion of his two parents, Joe doubted Bobby got away with a thing.

Emma turned back to Joe and just that quickly, a shield went up. She slid her hands into the pockets of her skirt and focused on his face, her expression pleasant and coolly distant. He didn't have to be a mind reader to know she was royally ticked off at him. "I've got the For Sale sign for your front yard in the trunk of my car," she informed him impersonally. "I thought you might want to put it up, since the open house is tomorrow."

Yes, he did, and he also wanted to find out what was bugging her now. Joe could tell by the wary look on Bobby's face that he knew something was up, too.

"I'll be right there to help you," Joe promised Emma. He checked out Bobby and the weights, warning, "Don't overdo."

"I won't. And thanks, Joe." Bobby smiled at him worshipfully, "for telling me all about the academy."

Again, Emma tensed. Without another word, she turned on her heel and strode purposefully back to the trunk of her car. She inserted the key in the lock with jerky, economical motions. Joe had the feeling if she had opened her mouth just then or tried to talk, she'd have spit nails.

"Is there a problem?" he asked, irritated by her show of temper when all he'd been doing was being nice to her son.

Emma opened the trunk lid and lifted the sign and a metal hammer out. "Why would there be a problem?" she snapped.

Joe wrested the metal realty sign from her grip and followed her over to the center of his front yard. "I don't know." He looked at the rigid set of her shoulders beneath the long, boxy suit jacket. "You tell me."

Emma's breasts raised and lowered with each deep, irritated breath she took. Color flooded her cheeks. "Why would I be annoyed? I mean what possible reason could I have, Joe? Just because you're trying to brainwash my son into thinking he needs to go to the gosh-darned Naval Academy—"

The academy meant everything to Joe. He wouldn't listen to anyone, including Emma, denigrate it. But sensing arguing the merits of the academy, citing all the discipline and superior education he had received there had done for him, would be a waste of breath where Emma was concerned, he countered only with, "Hey, I didn't bring the subject up. He did."

"But you were only too happy to try to recruit him to your way of life." Emma turned the sign so it was visible to traffic coming both ways on the suburban street. Bracing it with one hand, she used the hammer to begin pounding it into the ground.

Joe took the hammer from her and accomplished with four sharp strokes what it would have taken her twenty or more to do. "What's wrong with my way of life?" Dropping the heavy hammer to his side, he checked to make sure the sign was secure in the ground, and found to his satisfaction, and Emma's obvious irritation, that it was.

Her arms folded at her waist, Emma glared at him and, refusing to answer his question, said, "I want him to be happy, Joe. I want him to be safe, not out fighting some awful war."

Now it was Joe's turn to see red. "Right. As long as someone else's son, husband and father are doing the fighting it's okay, right, Emma? I thought attitudes like yours went out with Vietnam. Guess not." Having had enough of the conversation, he gave her the hammer back and marched toward the house.

"Joe—" Emma ran to catch up. He stood rigidly. "I'm sorry. I didn't mean to insult you."

Joe was so angry that he couldn't speak. Emma's attitude now was exactly as it had always been. And now she was trying to pass those same attitudes on to her son. "Don't apologize," he said through his teeth. "You feel how you feel."

"But maybe—" She took a deep breath, looking as if she felt guilty and contrite as hell. "I'm sorry, Joe. I shouldn't have said those things to you."

He didn't want an apology from her if what she felt in her heart hadn't changed. "But you still feel the same way," he probed.

"Of course I do!" she returned emotionally, her bright blue eyes shimmering with pent-up emotion. She stalked toward him. "I already lost one person I loved to the Navy. Do you really think I want to lose another?" Too late, she realized she had said more than she intended. And so did Joe. He had always felt that she loved him then, but to hear her admit it made the love they had felt then all the more real and tangible to him now.

Looking as if she were embarrassed beyond belief, Emma muttered a short, swift expletive and whirled.

Refusing to let her run off, Joe caught her arm. "Bobby will always love you," he reassured her softly. "No matter where he goes or what he does, he will always be your son. That won't change."

She looked at him uncertainly. Again, he had the fleeting feeling she was hiding something. What, he didn't know. And he wasn't sure he'd ever know.

EMMA WAS UP bright and early Saturday morning. The open house started at ten and ran until five. Because the property had just come out in yesterday's MLS listings book for the first time, she was expecting a run of real estate agents and prospective clients out to see Joe's house. And although she was excited about that, she wasn't excited about seeing Joe. Yesterday had been just too awkward. She should never have blown up at him for talking to Bobby about the academy, even if she didn't want Bobby to go there.

But she had blown up, and once she'd lost her temper, other things had come tumbling out...like the fact she'd once loved Joe, and wasn't over the loss of him yet. At least not deep down inside where it counted.

The more she was around him, the closer they got, the more disloyal and uncertain she felt. Her awkwardness only increased when she went over to his home and found him waiting for her.

"They did a nice job on the carpet," Emma remarked as she stepped inside.

"The tile, too."

Emma walked around, amazed at the transformation that had taken place in the short amount of time Joe had been back. "The house looks like new inside," she continued, pleased.

"I know." Joe glanced at his watch, his attitude abruptly as nervous and decidedly impersonal as her own. "So," he said, inhaling deeply, "when will the first agents arrive?"

"Soon," Emma promised, wondering what she'd been thinking when she agreed to list his house. "There's a caravan of them coming over from Century 21. And another from our office."

"Caravan?"

"Sorry," she apologized automatically, with a smile. "I keep thinking you know the lingo. A caravan's a big group of agents in cars, all going from one new listing to the next."

"Oh," Joe said. Again the conversation ran out of steam. Emma strode to the window, her heels sinking into the plush carpet she and Joe had picked out. She peered out through the gleaming windowpane, remarking, "You did a nice job on the glass, Joe. It really sparkles." *Much more of this and he's going to think I have the IQ of a gnat,* Emma thought.

"Just call me Mr. Clean," he said dryly.

Their glances meshed, held. *He's thinking about the kiss, about the way he wanted me and the way I responded.* Heat climbing into her face, Emma looked out at the empty street. *I want to make love with him again, too,* she realized with mixed feelings of wonder and despair as she recalled what it had been like to be in his arms again. *It would take so little effort on your part, Joe, for you to seduce me,* she thought. *And that makes me afraid. I don't want to be hurt again and I know you could hurt me even more now than you did years ago, when we were both eighteen.*

"Here's a car!" Joe said. "But it's Doris..."

Doris got out of the police sedan and walked up to the door. "Hi, Joe, Emma." She greeted them both officiously. "Got a minute?"

"Sure," Joe said, taking the initiative and answering for both of them as he ushered her inside. "What's up?"

Doris rested a palm on the nightstick at her waist. "We found the group of kids who've been breaking into the cars at the high school and we think they're the same ones who vandalized your property." She looked straight at Joe, her hazel eyes serious. "I need you to go down to the station and press charges against them. And Emma, I want you to go, too. You might be able to identify one of them."

"Now?" Emma asked, thinking this couldn't have happened at a more inopportune time.

Doris lifted both palms placatingly. "The sooner we can get the paperwork processed, the sooner we can move them over to juvenile hall."

Concerned, Joe turned to Emma. "What about the open house?" he asked.

"I'll call someone from my office to come over and stay here until we get back." She looked at Doris. "This isn't going to take long, is it?"

Doris shook her head. "I don't think so. We've already got one confession from a kid who wants to plea bargain. With you and Joe there, it'll only be a matter of time before the others begin to fold, too."

Unfortunately, the scene at the police station was every bit as tedious as Emma had anticipated. She was not able to positively identify anyone out of the lineup because it had been so dark and she'd been too far away to clearly see their faces. But just the fact the kids knew there was an adult there to look at them in the lineup sparked yet another confession, as well as a run-in with one of the marauding teenager's distraught mother that turned out to be very unpleasant.

"You can't press charges," the mother told Joe, tears steaming down her face. "You can't put my son in jail."

Joe turned to her, his face a cold mask of fury. "Do you have any idea what they did to my house?" he demanded.

"I know what they did was wrong. So do they. And I swear to you I'll see my son never comes near your house again—"

"They trashed it, lady," Joe went on as if the woman hadn't spoken.

"I know that, and I'm sorry. We'll pay for the damages. I'll make him get a job. Please, Mr. O'Reilly! Please don't do this. My son will get a criminal record!"

"After what he and his friends did to my house, your son deserves a criminal record," Joe said grimly.

Emma looked at the boy's mother and recognized her as one of the waitresses in a restaurant near the Northwestern campus. Softspoken and hardworking, she wore a faded cotton shirtdress and looked beaten down by life. *Had it not been for Skip, that might be me today,* Emma thought.

"He's my only son," the woman continued to sob, her work-worn hands digging into Joe's forearms. "He's all I have."

Even though she disapproved strongly of what the teen had done, Emma's heart went out to the woman. It was hard enough to rear a child with a husband to help out. She couldn't imagine trying to do it alone. And this woman wore no wedding ring.

Joe gently disengaged the woman's death grip on his arms. "I'm sorry," he said kindly but firmly. "But I didn't get your son into this mess. He did. And he's going to have to pay."

"If we could just settle this privately, out of court—"

"No." Joe turned to Emma, his manner brusque. "Ready to go?"

She nodded. They walked out to his Jeep in silence. Emma had never felt further away from Joe than she did at that moment.

"You think I'm wrong, don't you?" he surmised unhappily.

Emma couldn't bring herself to look at him, so she focused on the overcast gray sky instead. "I understand where the woman's coming from. If it were Bobby, I'd do the same thing."

"Then you'd be wrong," Joe said as he unlocked her side of the Jeep and opened the door for her.

She watched him circle around and climb in behind the wheel. Thinking there was still time to get him to change his mind, she touched his arm. "It's not wrong to want to protect someone you love, Joe."

His forearm remained stiff and inflexible beneath her coaxing touch. His mouth compressed tightly, he stared straight ahead. "It doesn't do kids any favor to make excuses for them. If my father hadn't made excuses for my sister's wild behavior, she would still be alive today." That said, he turned to face her.

Not knowing what to say to that, Emma was silent. She knew how much Mary's death had hurt him. It had torn him and his father apart. There was no way to fix that—ever.

"Whatever happens now will be the best thing that ever could have happened to the kid," Joe said firmly. "He's got to learn the consequences of what he did, and so does his mother. I won't bail him out. Period."

Emma was silent as she realized what a hard man Joe was. Something was either right or wrong to him. There was no middle ground.

A chill went down her back. If he ever found out how she had lied . . . He wouldn't.

She wouldn't let him.

EMMA WAS JUST PUTTING the finishing touches on her makeup Monday morning when she heard a ping against her bedroom window, followed swiftly by another, and then a few moments later, another. Still fastening her earrings, she walked to the window and saw Joe standing underneath.

One glance at his face, and she knew what he wanted. She sent him a stern glance. "I'm going to work, Joe."

He countered with another tossed juniper berry and a winning smile. "Play hookey with me."

Oh, if only I could, Emma thought wistfully. "I can't." Again, she kept her voice firm.

He moved closer, until she could see the tossed layers of his dark hair—which was getting longer and more rakish every day—and smell the clean soapy fragrance of his skin and hair. "Got a closing today?"

"No."

His grin widened a little more. "An appointment to show houses?" he probed.

"No."

He braced a brawny shoulder against the brick and continued to peer up at her intently. "Then what's keeping you from taking a day off?"

Ah, Emma thought, that was easy. "The mortgage that's due at the end of the month."

He regarded her sagely. His options were almost exhausted and he knew it; yet he wasn't giving up. Finally, he uttered a beleaguered sigh and said with mock seriousness, "This is all your fault, you know."

She arched a brow. "That you're bored, Joe O'Reilly? Somehow, I don't think so."

"Well, I do." Joe had no problem disagreeing. "You did such a good job helping me prepare my house for sale that the prospective buyers are driving me crazy. Every hour someone calls and wants to see it."

"That's good!"

"Not when I'm trying to watch a movie on TV. Or take a shower. Or fix something to eat."

She saw his point. Still, it was par for the course when you had a house on the market. "Joe, it's only been forty-eight hours," she chided gently, pushing up the screen so they could talk face-to-face. "I think you'll live."

"The longest forty-eight hours of my life," he lamented with an expression that was both comical and pitiable.

For her, too, Emma thought. But it hadn't been because his house was on the market. No, the forty-eight hours had been incredibly long and depressing because she and Joe hadn't really seen much of each other since they'd left the police station.

Fearing what would happen if she got too close to Joe and inadvertently let something of her deception slip, Emma had purposefully kept her distance from him. And had been lonely as hell.

"Just a few hours, Emma," Joe continued to persuade softly. "Just a walk along the lakeshore. What do you say?"

Emma looked longingly at the blue sky overhead and the bright sunshine-filled morning. The truth was, she could use some time off. She had worked all weekend and knew she would be working just as hard later in the week, when four of her current closings were scheduled. "Half a day," she said finally.

"Or a whole," Joe bargained.

Emma gave him a stern look, aware he could probably seduce her into anything if he put half a mind to it. "Don't press your luck," she warned softly, unable to completely suppress a smile.

"Does that mean you'll go?"

Emma looked into his golden brown eyes and suntanned face, aware she was fighting a losing battle and not minding so much anymore. He would only be here two more weeks. Then his leave would be up. The danger of discovery would be gone.

"Give me five minutes and I'll be right with you."

THE SAND WAS WARM beneath their feet as Joe and Emma walked barefoot on the shore along Lake Michigan. "It's like looking out at the ocean," Emma murmured as she studied the choppy blue-gray waves with the foaming white crests.

Joe resisted the urge to take her hand in his and shoved his fists into the pockets of his shorts instead. He had an idea she was still a little mad at him for pressing charges against that kid, but he wasn't going to change his mind. "I'd forgotten how much I missed the lake."

And until she'd cut him out of her life again, even for a couple of days, he'd forgotten how much he missed Emma when he couldn't see or talk to her. Until he'd come back, he hadn't realized how strong his feelings for her were. Now he knew. She was in his thoughts day and night. He got high watching her smile. Fighting with her—even about something stupid—was torture.

Like on Saturday, at the police station. He'd half expected to get grief from the negligent parents. He hadn't expected Emma to give him flak, too. But maybe he should have. He had known from the very first how softhearted she was. Over the years that hadn't changed. She always thought of others first.

"Bobby loves Lake Michigan, too," Emma murmured as she paused to admire a rainbow-striped sailboat gliding back and forth in the wind.

"He's a good kid," Joe said.

Emma turned to him with a generous smile. "The two of you have a nice rapport," she said, pleased.

Joe shrugged, seeing nothing remarkable about that. "He's easy to talk to, just like you are."

A funny look flashed across Emma's face, followed swiftly by what looked like guilt to Joe. Though what Emma would have to feel guilty about, he didn't know. "What's wrong?" he asked, wishing he didn't always feel so suspicious about her, deep down. But then, what could he expect, remembering how she had betrayed him before.

"Nothing." She turned so he couldn't see her face.

Hands on her shoulders, he spun her gently around to face him. He hated it when she looked troubled and then shut him out like this. "What's on your mind, Emma? What's bothering you?"

She shook her head, unwilling to confess. "It's stupid."

"I won't laugh," he promised gently, thinking how nice it was to be out here with her, like this.

She took a deep unsteady breath and prepared to confess. "I was just thinking...wondering, really...what it would have been like all those years ago if you and I had eloped instead of Skip and I."

Her words jolted him, but they weren't entirely un-expected. Joe had wondered, too, especially after spending time with Bobby and seeing what a great loving mother Emma had turned out to be. He was all too aware that had he chosen not to go into the academy that Bobby would very likely be his kid. And Emma, his wife.

But there was no point dwelling on it. Their lives hadn't followed that path. Deciding to get them out of this trench they'd dug themselves into, he teased, "I think if we'd married we'd have about six kids by now—"

Emma arched a disbelieving brow. "In twelve years?"

The thought of making love to Emma time after time made him hard, mainly because she had always been so responsive. Joe picked up the pace of their walk and willed his erection to go away. "Sounds good to me."

"Sounds like a handful," Emma corrected.

"So?" Joe figured life was nothing without a challenge. "We'd be adept at handling all crises."

"Or be in a crisis," Emma teased. She sobered abruptly. "You really should marry, Joe."

He looked at her long and hard and said simply, "I plan to."

Chapter Ten

"Mom, you're never going to believe it! I was invited to Sandy Jardine's graduation party!"

"Who's Sandy Jardine?" Emma asked. She was in the garage, getting out the fertilizer. She had promised Joe she would help him care for his bushes, now that all of them were pruned.

"Just the coolest girl in my class," Bobby responded as he paced excitedly back and forth. "Anyway, she's having a party Friday night and I'm invited!"

"Congratulations," Joe said, coming into the garage. He looked more tanned than ever after another day spent in the sun. Emma had never seen anyone with a healthier glow about him, and the impact of his presence hit her like an arrow to the heart. Judging by the warm, intense look on his face, Joe felt the same. He had wanted to kiss her out on the beach. He hadn't. There was no guaranteeing how long his iron self-control would last, though. No guaranteeing how she would respond if he did kiss her. She wished she could say she would let it go no further than a simple kiss, but she wasn't sure that was true any longer. Even knowing he was leaving again—soon—she still wanted to be with him.

Joe's eyes met Emma's and he smiled before looking back at Bobby. "So what are you going to do at this party?"

"I don't know." Bobby shrugged. "Eat, drink, be merry and celebrate the end of junior high, I guess. What do people usually do at boy-girl parties, Joe?"

"Depends on the guys and gals, I imagine," Emma said, reexerting some control over her son. She knew Bobby liked Joe and looked up to him enormously, but she was still the parent here. "Speaking of which," Emma continued matter-of-factly, "I'm going to have to call Sandy's parents and make sure the party is going to be properly chaperoned."

"Mom!" Bobby looked horrified. He turned to Joe for help.

"She's right," Joe put in before Bobby could protest further, and Emma sent him a grateful glance. "Besides, all parents do that nowadays," Joe continued knowledgeably.

Bobby sighed heavily. Ignoring her son's glum expression, Joe continued, "So, what are you going to wear?"

Bobby's fair brows drew together. "Good question," he said, perplexed, then looked at Joe again for help. "You're a guy. What do you think I should wear? The invitation said casual. She's got a pool and there might be some swimming if it's warm enough."

"It's a cookout, then?" Joe asked as soon as he could get a word in edgewise.

Bobby nodded. "In their backyard."

"Why don't you ask your dad?" Joe suggested tactfully. "Skip's always been a very sharp dresser. I'm sure he knows what's cool and what's not."

"Yeah, you're right. Dad does have good taste in clothes and stuff," Bobby said, breathing an enormous sigh of relief. He looked at Emma. "Do you mind if I call him right now?"

"Not at all. Try his office first, though. I think he has office hours over at the university this evening."

Bobby darted out of the garage.

"That was nice of you," Emma said, stacking her spade, gardening gloves and fertilizer in a red wagon that had once been Bobby's but was now used to cart stuff around.

"What was nice?" Joe moved forward to give her a hand lifting the heavy sack into the wagon.

"Referring Bobby to Skip," she said as they inadvertently brushed shoulders and a tingle of warmth arrowed down her arm.

"What do I know about clothes? I'm always in jeans or a T-shirt when I'm not in uniform."

Joe's taste might go to the classic, but he knew precisely what colors to buy, and as for styles, there was nothing, it seemed, that wouldn't positively accentuate the rugged masculinity of his tall frame. Emma had no doubt he could outfit Bobby with similar ease. But he hadn't, because he knew in his heart that it would be best for Bobby to get that kind of help from Skip.

But there were also things, like his introduction to the weights, boxing gloves and a punching bag, that he could have gotten only from Joe. Emma knew that because of Joe's continuing interest in Bobby and the general buddying around they had done, Bobby's self-image was much stronger than it had been. For that, she and Bobby both owed him a lot. And she realized just as swiftly, what she wanted to give him in thanks. It didn't matter that Joe could hardly be expected to understand the significance of such an event. She would know what a special gift it was.

"Speaking of Bobby's graduation from junior high," she said, "they're passing out the diplomas in a special ceremony at Bobby's school on Friday afternoon." She paused. As she looked into his eyes and saw the deepening affection and interest there, she found the courage to go on, to ask what once would have been impossible. "I know it would mean a lot to him, Joe, if you were there, too."

EMMA AND JOE were almost done with his roses when Bobby returned from his impromptu shopping jaunt with Skip. Excited about his purchases, he came straight back to Joe's backyard, with Skip following casually behind. "Hey, Mom! Joe! Look what Dad got for me!" Bobby pulled a neon bright T-shirt and jams from a Marshall Field's bag and held them up for their perusal. "And I got some new swim trunks, too," Bobby said, pulling those out, "just in case."

"That's great!" Emma said, sending Skip an approving glance.

"You'll be the coolest guy there," Joe confirmed, also impressed.

Bobby smiled, looking impossibly young and grown up all at once. "I'm going to go in and call Toby," he announced to one and all before darting off.

Emma watched him go in amusement, very aware her son never walked anywhere when he could run. When would that change? she wondered. And would she be sad when it did?

She looked at Skip, who was thoughtfully regarding Joe's and Emma's grimy, post-gardening state. Though his expression was carefully neutral, Emma knew what he was thinking. Skip was wondering whether she was loyal to him or to Joe first. Two weeks ago the answer would have been easy. Now she just felt torn between the two men. She owed them both in so many ways. And Skip knew that, too. That Joe was bending over backward not to usurp Skip's position with Bobby made her hopeful. Maybe, Emma thought, pleased, with careful handling there could be room for all of them in Bobby's life.

"Thanks for taking Bobby shopping," she said to Skip, knowing he'd saved her not just a trip to the mall but several hours of browsing and debating, too. These days, Bobby just couldn't quite trust her judgment in clothing. Or in other words, if his mother liked it, there must be something wrong with it.

"My pleasure," Skip replied.

Despite the heat of the evening and the rigors of shopping with an eleven-year-old boy, Skip looked cool and sophisticated in his tailored slacks, shirt and tie. His gaze genial, he looked at Joe and said with quiet thanks. "Bobby's told me what you've been doing for him, Joe. The weight set and all. It brings back a lot of memories."

"Yeah." Joe smiled cautiously, holding Skip's gaze with more friendliness than he'd had for him since he'd returned to Evanston. "It does, doesn't it?"

A comfortable silence fell between the three of them, and again, Emma felt a flare of hope.

"I was telling Emma earlier what a good job the two of you had done rearing him," Joe continued appreciatively. "He's a nice kid."

"Thanks," Skip said, looking pleased before finishing with a paternal pride that had Emma squirming, "I think so."

Oh, Joe, Emma thought unhappily, as a new wave of guilt made her wonder for the thousandth time that month if she was doing the right thing in adhering to the secrets of the past. Or if she should reconsider, and somehow convince Skip it was time for them to find a way to make this situation right. The truth was, she didn't know how much longer she could live with the lie, because she was beginning to see that she owed Joe, too.

Again, she looked at Joe, who was so completely innocent and unaware of their duplicity. *You don't know what we did to you. You think you do but the reality is you don't even know the half of it....*

"WITHOUT A DOUBT, this was the worst idea you ever had," Skip told Emma at the reception following Bobby's graduation.

As much as Emma hated to admit it, she had to agree with him. This had been a bad idea. She had been miserable sitting between Joe and Skip all during the ceremony. Not that Joe had done anything to make her uncomfortable. On the contrary, he had bent over backward to be genial. It was Skip who had reacted by being both jealous and difficult. And those emotions were magnified a hundredfold as he watched Bobby across the cafeteria, leading Joe around and introducing him to all his friends.

"He's loving it, isn't he?" Skip said angrily as he downed his punch.

Praying Skip wouldn't make a scene in front of the other parents, Emma said stiffly, "I think Joe enjoyed watching Bobby graduate." As she would have, had she not felt trapped in a romantic triangle that by all rights should have ended years ago. Her eyes taking in the hero worship of the circle of boys around Joe as he told stories about his part in Operation Desert Storm, she sipped her punch.

"I mean playing the returning war hero," Skip countered with resentful emphasis.

"Joe *is* a returning war hero," Emma replied.

Skip was silent. As Emma continued to glare at him, he admitted guiltily, "All right, that much was uncalled for on my part." He gave her a sharp look. "But you shouldn't have invited him here, Emma. Today should have been for the three of us—period."

Emma looked at him meaningfully, letting him know how she felt with a single glance. Although they had yet to actually discuss it, Skip had to know that she had invited Joe there not so much because she wanted him by her side, but because she felt she owed it to him. And to Bobby.

"It can't be easy for Bobby having his divorced parents here with dates," Skip continued plaintively.

Her patience fading fast, Emma sent him an exasperated look. "I'm the only person who brought someone, and Joe isn't a date," she said.

"Tell that to him," Skip retorted dourly.

Emma blushed. Skip was right. Joe did look at her with a certain...possessive intent. And though since he had been back they had only kissed that once, she felt, deep inside, it was only a matter of time before something more happened between them.

Pushing the beckoning image of her and Joe making love from her mind, Emma countered with as much calmness and tact as she could muster. "This is not bothering Bobby, Skip. He wants Joe here, and after all Joe's done for him the past couple of weeks in terms of raising Bobby's self-esteem, I think it's the least we can do."

A muscle twitched in Skip's jaw and he looked away. A gleam of moisture appeared in his eyes, but when he turned back to her, his jaw was set, his tone deathly quiet. "This isn't about the past couple of weeks and you know it, Emma."

Aware of the truth in his words, she was guiltily silent.

Skip drew a long breath and looked deep into her eyes. "I thought we had decided on a course of action years ago, Emma, when Bobby was just a baby."

"We did." She agreed readily about that much.

"But?" he prodded impatiently, wanting, needing her to tell him what had changed.

Emma looked back at Joe and Bobby, who were clearly so happy together, and knew in her heart it was past time she and Skip came to terms with what they had done, as well as what they both knew, even if Skip wasn't quite ready to admit it yet, they had to do in the future. "But...everything's different now," she continued quietly, determined to convince him of the same.

Skip grasped her arm and steered her farther out of earshot of others. "The hell it is, Emma!" he seethed in a tone barely above a whisper. "You made me a promise. Just like I made you one. That we were in this forever."

"And yet we managed to divorce, anyway," Emma pointed out archly, irritated he was being so selfish.

Skip flinched. Unable to deny that he had wanted their divorce as much as she, unable to deny his relief when they no longer had to feign a passion that had never, ever existed, he was grimly silent.

Without warning, Joe was crossing the room to their sides. "Everything okay over here?" he asked cheerfully, giving Emma a sharp assessing look that missed absolutely nothing.

Emma smiled brightly and, because she had to, lied through her teeth. "Everything's fine," she said cheerfully. "Bobby, did you get some cookies?"

"Not yet."

She smiled even harder, forcing normalcy into her voice. "Why don't you take Joe through the line?" she suggested. She had never felt more trapped and miserable than she did at that very moment.

"Okay. C'mon, Joe. We better go before all that's left is *health food*."

Joe gave Emma a hard look, glanced at Skip, then moved to follow Bobby, his expression as deliberately cheerful as Emma's. And, she thought with a new wave of trepidation, just as false. Undoubtedly, she had some explaining to do to Joe, too; he wasn't about to let her off the hook. Dishonesty was something he simply would not tolerate from his friends, or from anyone.

As soon as they were gone, Skip picked up where they had left off. "You're letting your feelings for Joe cloud your judgment, Emma."

Wishing Skip would at least give her a chance to catch her breath, Emma edged around the perimeter of the cafeteria. "I don't have any feelings for Joe, other than friendship."

"Don't lie to me, Emma," Skip warned, intent on protecting his interests in this mess.

Emma glared at him, feeling ridiculously close to tears. And yet she understood all too well why Skip was reacting as he was. If she were in his position, faced with the possibility of losing his son to another man, she would probably fight fiercely, too.

"We made decisions in the past," Skip continued, his voice dropping to a low persuasive murmur. "Right or wrong, you and I got married. We made decisions we felt were for the best. We have to adhere to those decisions."

"Even if we know those decisions are wrong?" Emma whispered back and had the satisfaction of seeing Skip flinch uncertainly. Her lower lip trembled with the effort it was taking to check the wellspring of tumultuous emotions inside her. All too aware of the way Skip had stood by her, when not many other men would have, she continued with heartfelt sincerity, "Skip, I love you and I always will. You know that, but I'm no longer sure we have the right to keep the truth from Joe. Every time I see the two of them together..." She shook her head, tortured by the knowledge of what they'd done in their innocence. "Joe was our friend, Skip. Our good friend. He still is."

"He won't be our friend for long if he finds out what we did," Skip predicted direly. His hand closed over Emma's, warmly and reassuringly this time as the friendship they had shared over the years reasserted itself. "Look, I know how you feel," he said softly, his gray eyes beseeching her to listen. "I've been feeling guilty and confused, too. Especially since the whole reason we both got involved in this situation was because we both loved Joe so much and we wanted to protect him and help him out—"

Emma closed her eyes. What Skip was saying was true. They had been trying to protect Joe, but she knew now they never should have lied. Now that Joe was back, now that he was getting close to her again, and even to Bobby and Skip, they couldn't keep up the deception. Not and live with themselves later. And the more time went on, the worse their betrayal got. Surely Skip had to realize that, too, she thought desperately. "We should tell him the truth now—"

"No!" Skip's voice cut across hers sharply. "He would never understand and you know it."

Stung by the unaccustomed harshness in Skip's voice, Emma took a step back, away from him. Unbidden, she recalled Joe's quarrels with his father, the grudge he had held against him until the very day his father died. She thought of Joe in the police station, coldly refusing to cut the marauding teen's mother any slack. She sighed sadly and tears of futility and hopelessness stung her eyes.

Skip was right. To Joe there was right and there was wrong. And Emma knew he would think what they had done was wrong.

JOE WAS only half listening to Bobby's tales about the annual floor-hockey tournament in the gym the month before as they went through the refreshment line. He was watching Emma and Skip. In a corner by the stage, they were still whispering. About what, he had no idea. He only knew that Emma looked more torn and miserable than he'd ever seen her, and Skip more pressured—and just as miserable and fearful as Emma. Something was going on between them, something they didn't want him to know about.

This shouldn't bother him. Emma and Skip had been married once, after all. They were still rearing a child together. It was natural they'd want to talk privately. But it wasn't natural for Skip to be pressuring Emma the way he was. It wasn't natural for her to look so tense or send Joe on his way with a falsely cordial smile.

He couldn't shake the feeling they were in collusion about something. That being the case, he wondered how much he could trust Emma—or Skip. All he knew was that it hurt, watching them whisper together and deliberately shut him out.

"THANKS FOR COMING to Bobby's graduation, Joe," Skip said.

For Bobby's sake, Joe decided to ignore the hush-hush dramatics he had witnessed between Skip and Emma and respond with the expected cordiality. "It was my pleasure," Joe said, thinking Skip couldn't have given him a more potent brush-off if he'd tried. They both knew Skip wanted to get rid of him, and as soon as possible.

"And my pleasure, too," Bobby added, reaching out to shake Joe's hand.

Skip looked at Joe. "Emma and I are taking Bobby over to my folks' for a family dinner."

"And then I'm on to Sandy's party," Bobby reported, still glowing with the excitement of the day. He high-fived Joe. "Wish me luck, dude."

Joe shook his head and regarded Bobby fondly as he reminded him, "You don't need luck, remember? You've got brains and charm."

"Yeah, I do, don't I?" Bobby grinned without a hint of modesty. And all the adults laughed.

Joe congratulated Bobby one more time on his graduation, then watched Emma and Skip depart with their son. And as he did, a feeling of sadness overwhelmed him. Bobby was a great kid. He would miss him when he left.

As for Emma . . . Joe sighed heavily. About Emma, he didn't know what to think.

"MAYBE WE SHOULD TALK some more," Skip said, as he parked his car in Emma's driveway.

"No, Skip. We said more than enough at the reception." As long as she lived, she would never forget the look on Joe's face. Whatever trust he had regained in her in the past two weeks had been lost in the space of minutes. And for that, she was unbearably sad. Even if she wanted to, she knew she couldn't explain, not without making everything that much worse. And things were already bad enough.

"I'm sorry I was angry," Skip said quietly.

Now he calms down enough to be reasonable, Emma thought.

"But you have to admit you've given me reason."

For the scene he'd caused at the graduation? Emma didn't think so. But figuring they'd argued enough, she said only, "Good night, Skip."

He leaned across to talk to her through the open car door. "You want Bobby to call you when I pick him up at eleven?"

"If he wants," Emma said tiredly, speaking to Skip over her shoulder. "Otherwise, I'll hear all about the party when you bring him home tomorrow morning."

As was his custom, Skip waited until she was safely in the house before he backed out of the drive. No sooner had his car gone, then Emma heard footsteps moving across her porch. Peering through the portal, she saw Joe. He was dressed in the same shirt, tie and sport coat he'd worn earlier in the day. He looked anything but understanding and patient.

Her heart beating crazily, she slowly opened the door.

He looked her straight in the eye. "We have to talk."

Emma knew they did, and suddenly, she didn't know whether to laugh or cry. She walked wearily over to the sofa and, kicking off her shoes, curled up on one end of it. "That's all anyone seems to want today," she said.

He sat down on the opposite end of her sofa and studied her. "I don't like being shut out, Emma."

She turned her glance from his intent golden brown gaze. "I don't like being grilled." *Especially when I know I can't tell you the truth, no matter how much I want to.*

"You dismissed me like an errant schoolboy this afternoon."

She knew what he was talking about. He was talking about her sending him to get his punch and cookies in the cafeteria. "I'm sorry," she returned dryly, wishing they could talk about anything but her argument with Skip. "Next time I'll let you decide when to get your own punch and cookies."

He looked at her as if she was a stranger, and in many ways, considering all she couldn't tell him, she felt as if she was. "What's wrong with you?" he demanded.

Nothing that a complete memory loss wouldn't cure, Emma thought with bitter irony. Aware of a building pressure above her eyes, she massaged her temples. "Joe, I'm tired." *Tired of all the lies. Tired of beating myself up for my past mistakes. Tired of having you think the worst of me and knowing there's nothing I can do about it, nothing, without hurting you even more.*

"I'm tired, too," he said quietly, his tone low and insistent. "I'm tired of being kept in the dark."

Tears gathered in the corners of her eyes. Emma shut her lashes and struggled not to let them fall. "I'm sorry you feel that way."

Joe made no comment on the thickened, emotional timbre of her low tone, but she knew he was every bit as aware of it as she.

"That's all the explanation you're going to give me?" he asked, hurt.

It's all I can. Nevertheless, Emma knew she had to tell him something. He wouldn't give up until she did. "Skip and I were arguing today, okay?"

"About me?" Joe's tone said he wasn't happy about that, either.

"Yes. He didn't think I should've invited you to Bobby's graduation. He felt it was awkward and inappropriate."

It was Joe's turn to look guilty and uncomfortable. "Maybe you shouldn't have invited me."

Emma's head lifted sharply. "Skip does not dictate who I see," she countered sharply.

Joe's dark brow arched in disbelief. "It looked that way today. In fact it looked like he has *quite* a hold on you," he said, "despite your divorce."

Her patience exhausted, Emma was on her feet. She didn't need this. She didn't need any of it. "Get out," she ordered, pushing the words through her teeth. *Before I say things we'll both regret.*

Joe stood but made no move to go. "Not before I have the answer to one thing." He stalked nearer and tucked a hand beneath her chin, lifting her face so she couldn't possibly avoid his assessing glance. "Are you still in love with him, Emma?"

Emma was trembling from head to toe, as much from exhaustion as fear of discovery. She jerked her head from his compelling grasp and paced a distance away. "No."

He studied her a long time, not arguing with her, but not quite believing things were that simple, either. "Were you ever?" he asked finally in a voice laced with bitter remonstration.

Emma knew to tell him the truth about that would be to tell him too much. Besides, she still had Bobby to protect. And Bobby couldn't know anything of this. In his vulnerable state, the knowledge would destroy him.

"Then why did you marry him?" Joe asked in a hoarse whisper, having already jumped to his own conclusions. He stepped nearer and took her by the arms. "Did you want to get back at me that badly?"

No, Emma thought, as the warmth from his hands penetrated through her clothes to her skin. *I wanted to protect you, Joe.* But knowing Joe would never understand that, never in a million years, she simply shook her head and, extricating herself graciously from his light grasp once again, wordlessly showed him to the door.

And once there, she knew what had to be said. Like it or not, there were secrets that still had to be kept. For now and maybe forever. "The past is over, Joe," she said wearily in a voice that was ragged with pain, her hand clutching the doorknob until it ground into the palm of her hand. "For all our sakes, please, let it be over!"

Chapter Eleven

"Mom, good news!" Bobby said early the following morning as he strode in the back door. "Dad's taking me to Washington D.C.!"

Skip followed Bobby into Emma's kitchen. "I was asked to present a paper I've written at Georgetown University."

Emma paused, the breakfast dishes she was doing all but forgotten. "Again? That's the third time this year, isn't it?"

"Yeah, it is." Skip smiled proudly.

Sensing something more was up by the widening of Skip's grin and the excited gleam in his eyes, she wiped her hands on a dish towel and prodded, "And?"

"And they've offered me a job in their economics department."

Emma's heart slammed to a stop. Forcing her voice to remain neutral, she asked, "Are you going to take it?" No one was more aware than she how much she still depended on Skip to help her out with Bobby, or how much Bobby depended on his Dad to be there for him, not just occasionally, but on a daily basis.

"It's tempting," Skip admitted with a nonchalant shrug, then hesitated. He looked at her candidly. "It's an excellent career opportunity. It would mean, among other things, a substantial pay raise, but it would also mean I'd have to move to Washington, and be away from you and Bobby. And that's something I don't want." The corners of his mouth turned down seriously. "I like the custody arrangement we have, Emma. I don't want a new one."

"I don't, either," Bobby interrupted, then heaved a relieved sigh as he realized his dad wasn't going to move away, after all. "If you lived in D.C., I'd hardly ever get to see you."

Skip wrapped a paternal arm around Bobby's shoulders. "Precisely why I can't take the job. But I have agreed to give a number of seminars there, as many as I can fit in my schedule. The first is this next week. And since you're out of school now, I thought it'd be a good time to take you to see the Capitol. That is, if your mom agrees, of course."

"Of course Bobby can go with you," Emma said.

"Cool!" Bobby interrupted enthusiastically as he opened the refrigerator and pulled out a container of chocolate milk. "Can we go to the Smithsonian? And the White House?"

"We'll see everything you want," Skip promised, looking pleased.

Emma watched Bobby splash some milk into a glass. He was looking so grown up these days, so confident and male. He even walked with a bit of a derring-do stride now. "When would the two of you have to leave?" she asked, her mind already gearing up to practical matters like packing and wardrobe planning.

"This afternoon," Skip said.

That didn't give them much time, Emma thought. "How long are you staying?" Out of the corner of her eye, she watched Bobby pour himself a second glass of milk and then drink every last drop of it.

"A week," Skip continued. "We'll be back next Sunday."

The ramifications of that did not escape her. Skip and Bobby would return the day before Joe was scheduled to leave, Emma thought. Which meant they'd have very little if any time left to spend with each other. But considering the fight at the graduation, the tug of war that was starting over her and her son, maybe Skip's plan was best, Emma thought. Certainly, it would take some of the stress out of her life. Noting that Bobby was waiting with bated breath for her reaction to their plans, Emma smiled at him and said, "It sounds like a wonderful opportunity." She watched Bobby beam right back at her. "I guess we'd better get you packed."

Bobby rushed to put his glass in the sink, then cut her off at the pass. "I can do it myself, Mom. I'm not a little kid anymore, you know."

JOE WAS in the front yard, painting the mailbox when Doris drove up. "Cheer up," she said as she got out of her car and circled around to greet him. "All this hard work will be done soon."

Joe knew. In a little over a week he was going to be leaving again. It was going to be harder this time than it had been when he left for the academy, maybe because there were still so many things unresolved. He hadn't had nearly enough time with Emma. He would miss seeing her in the future. And Bobby, too. He hadn't known the little guy long but already he felt remarkably close to him. "So what's up?" Joe asked, stroking white paint up and down the wooden base.

"A colleague of mine down at the station wants to see the house. Her parents are retiring to Evanston to be near her. They've already sold their place in Decatur, so they need quick possession. Your house would be perfect for them."

Joe sat back on his haunches, unable to resist teasing, "You're really trying to get me out of here, aren't you?"

"You know me better than that. I'm going to miss you like crazy." Doris paused. She hunkered down beside him and searched his face. "Is it true, what I heard about you and Emma?"

"I don't know," he said nonchalantly, ignoring the way his gut tightened just hearing Emma's name. "What'd you hear?"

Doris brushed a lock of auburn hair from her forehead. "That the two of you might be an item again. That she's always over here—"

"She listed my house."

"Or you're always over there."

"As I said," Joe replied with a great deal more patience than he felt, "she listed my house."

Doris grinned, not buying that for a moment. "And you went to Bobby's graduation," she continued.

"As a friend," Joe corrected.

Doris's hazel eyes glowed with speculative lights. "I'm a friend. I wasn't invited."

Joe resumed painting. "I take it you've been talking to Skip."

Doris stood again and shoved both hands into the pockets of her uniform pants. "He's a little jealous. Emma hasn't dated anyone seriously since they divorced. And she's never looked at anyone the way she looks at you."

Joe found that hard to believe. He stood next to Doris and dropped his paintbrush in the empty can. "Not even Skip?"

"Not even Skip." Doris let that information sink in a bit before she continued as ruthlessly as ever, "So what's the scoop, Joe. Are you still in love with her?"

Was he? He'd almost lost Emma once because he hadn't fought hard enough. He knew deep down as much as he didn't want to admit it that he still wanted her, loved her.

Unfortunately, nothing was simple. Skip was still in the picture. They had Bobby to consider. He had very little time left here and no real vacation for another year. Then there was Emma and Skip's guilt about the way they'd betrayed him, and the sense sometimes they were still in collusion.

He didn't want to be in the middle of a triangle any more than Emma did. On the other hand, her marriage to Skip had failed a long time ago. If not for Bobby, he doubted the two of them would be nearly as close as they were now.

"I take it you're not going to answer me," a frustrated Doris presumed after a moment.

"You take it right," Joe said amiably.

"You always were a hard man to read, Joe O'Reilly."

Not where Emma was concerned. There, he'd always worn his heart on his sleeve. And maybe that was the problem. He'd never loved anyone the way he loved Emma and he knew now he never would.

"So what do you think?" Joe asked Emma after the Kosteleckys had left.

"They liked it. They liked it a lot."

"But?"

"But whether they put a bid on it or not will depend on what else they've seen," Emma explained. "We'll just have to wait it out."

Silence stretched between them, broken only by the sounds of the summer breeze blowing in through the open windows and the sounds of a neighbor mowing his lawn farther down the street. "Bobby and Skip get off to Washington okay?" Joe paced to the window. Looking out, he could see the freshly painted mailbox gleaming whitely in the sun.

"Yes," Emma replied, beginning to gather up her things and prepare to leave, too. "They left a little while ago. They're going to call me tonight from the hotel, just to let me know they arrived safely."

She snapped her briefcase shut just as the phone rang. Reluctantly, Joe left her side and went to get it. Not surprisingly, it wasn't for him. "It's for you, Emma." He handed the receiver to her.

As he watched, Emma listened for several moments, her expression both calm and intent. For the hundredth time since he had been back, Joe found himself thinking what a truly beautiful woman she was. Her long hair was perfect, so soft and silky and healthy and honey blond. Her clothes were flawless, too, both elegant and chic. Although, he admitted to himself, with her slender waist and hips, perfect breasts and legs that went on forever, she would have looked good in a sackcloth.

"Well, I'll convey the offer," Emma said finally, "but I don't know how he'll react. He's put so much work into this place. I think he really wants to get top dollar. Yes, I know. All right. Talk to you soon."

"What?" Joe asked, the second she'd hung up.

Emma turned to face him, looking not at all pleased. "That was the sales agent for the Kosteleckys. They've made a bid ten percent lower than the asking price, Joe."

Joe crossed his arms over his chest and watched as her teeth raked her lower lip. "Do you think I can get the asking price?"

Emma's chin went up determinedly. She walked closer. "Yes, I do," she said firmly, the timbre of her low, sexy voice dropping as she neared. "If you're willing to wait. If you're not . . . well, it's up to you."

Joe was silent. Three weeks ago, he probably would have jumped at the offer—any offer. Now, he didn't know. Suddenly, he wasn't in near the rush to sell as he had been, and his feelings had nothing to do with the state of the current real estate market.

Misunderstanding the reason for his hesitation, Emma continued frankly, "It's another ten thousand dollars, Joe. You don't have to rush to decide. In fact,

I think you should take your time—at least twenty-four hours—and think about it."

Joe shook his head. "I don't have to think about it," he countered, meeting her bright blue gaze head-on. Emma was right. He had done a hell of a lot of work on this place. "I'm not taking the offer," he continued flatly. "I want the asking price and not a penny less."

Emma grinned, looking every bit as pleased with him as she was with herself. Apparently, she appreciated a person with guts. "May I use your phone?"

Joe made a sweeping gesture toward it. "Please."

"Well, the other agent is definitely not a happy camper," Emma said long minutes later, after she'd hung up the phone again. "She says she doesn't know if her clients can come up with that much money." She paused, surveying him from head to toe, then frowned in puzzlement. "You don't look very unhappy about all this," she said, perplexed.

Joe shrugged, realizing he wasn't. "Something else will come up," he said confidently. And in the meantime, they had the rest of the weekend in front of them. No Bobby, no Skip.

Realizing both were at loose ends, at least he hoped Emma was, he asked casually, "Want to go out and celebrate *almost* selling my house?"

Emma grinned, amused, but before she could answer him the phone rang again. Joe nodded. "You might as well get it. We both know it's not for me."

With a sheepish grin, Emma picked it up. She listened intently, then broke into an even bigger smile. "I'll relay it. Yes. As soon as I can." She hung up and turned to face him, still beaming. "You're not going to believe it. They've countered again—with the full asking price!"

Reacting purely on instinct, Joe picked her up and spun her around until her feet left the floor. Too late, he realized the sensual impact of having her in his arms, her soft full breasts crushed against his chest, her slim thighs molded to his, and higher, the unmistakable evidence of his desire. She drew in her breath swiftly.

He knew she was shocked. So was he.

And just as unable to do anything about it.

Able to feel her resistance, he let her down slowly, and as he did, the lithe weight of her body glided unavoidably down the length of his. The trembling he felt in her body increased. Her knees were shaking slightly as she gave him a faltering smile.

Her palms on his forearms, Emma steadied herself and returned them to the very important business at hand. "But they want you to pay half of the closing costs," she said as she backed off. She pulled down her suit jacket, so it fell evenly at the trim line of her hips.

Joe tried not to think about the warm softness of her breasts beneath her silk blouse, the perfumed scent of her skin and hair or how naturally and perfectly the contours of her slim body meshed with his. It didn't matter that she smelled like the roses they had worked on in his yard, or that her lips were soft and lightly glossed to a pale peach shade very much like her own skin. *Think about the house, not how much you want to make love to her again.* "I think that's fair," he said.

Emma turned away from him, her tone brisk. "They want to sign the contract and put down earnest money today. If it's all right with you, we could go over to my office and do it now."

His mood suddenly as businesslike as hers, Joe nodded his assent.

"The other agent said they're paying cash, so we won't have to wait for a mortgage approval," Emma continued, gathering up her things. "That'll help speed things up."

The only problem was, Joe thought as he followed her out the door and locked up behind them, that he didn't want to speed things up. He wanted a reason to stay.

EMMA TYPED IN the last few words, then rolled the contract out of the typewriter. She glanced over it to make sure everything was correct, then joined the others in one of the realty office conference rooms and handed it to the other agent. Joe read it next. Then the Kosteleckys. The five of them worked out a closing date and all other relevant details pertaining to the sale. When they were finished, everyone shook hands.

"Well, I guess that's it," Joe said after the others had left the conference room. To Emma's surprise, he looked restless and irritable, rather than relieved and happy as she would have expected, but then she had an idea how he felt. The idea of his moving away permanently, of the two of them no longer being neighbors, saddened her, too.

"To the contrary, Joe. We're far from finished," Emma continued as she organized the papers in the file on his house. "The land will have to be surveyed, the house inspected. We have to contact an attorney and set up the closing for the end of next week, before you leave. It's going to be a busy week."

Joe looked no happier about that than he had been about the sale. "Don't worry," Emma reassured him calmly, hoping "seller's remorse" hadn't already set in. "I'll walk you through this every step of the way." She smiled in an effort to coax him back into a good mood. "That's what you're paying me for."

Joe nodded, still looking sad and uneasy.

"Second thoughts?" she asked, figuring if he had them they might as well deal with them now.

"I think it's just now hit me what I'm doing." The look in his eyes grew distant and he took a deep breath. "I'm not going to have a home here anymore."

Reminded of that, Emma felt as if she was going to cry. Struggling to contain her tears, she had no easy words of comfort for Joe that wouldn't in turn reveal her own distress.

"I guess it's going to be harder to leave this place than I thought," Joe continued quietly, after a moment, his tone reflective, his gaze sadder still.

Harder for her, too. *Stop it,* Emma commanded herself sternly. *You knew this was coming.*

Not about to cry and carry on the way she had the last time he'd had to leave her for the Navy, Emma put on a cheerful, professional facade. "Hey, enough of the sad faces," she chided him with every ounce of spirit she had. Pretending his leaving meant nothing to her, she approached him cheerfully, "We just sold your house, and in record time, no less! We should be celebrating."

Joe studied her and smiled. "You're right, of course," he countered lightly, looking deep into her eyes. "Enough of doom and gloom. How about dinner? My place?"

Emma hesitated. She wanted to go, so very much, but just the memory of being held in Joe's arms sent her senses spinning. Was it tempting fate to be alone with him in so intimate a setting?

"You've done so many wonderful things for me," Joe continued to persuade, the kindness in his eyes and the softness of his voice letting her know she had nothing to fear where he was concerned. Nothing would happen she didn't want to happen. "I want to pay you back," he continued casually.

The question was, Emma thought, more flustered than ever, what did she want to happen? A love affair with Joe and all the complex problems and continuing deceit that would bring? Or a safe, dull life without him? Unable to think clearly when he was that near to her, she shrugged off his offer shyly. "You don't owe me anything, Joe," she pointed out quietly. "I've just been doing my job."

"Yeah, well, I think I do owe you. Besides," he approached her offhandedly, "I want to make dinner for you."

She was being ridiculous. And perhaps egotistical as well. He had said dinner, not seduction. Emma picked up her briefcase and headed for the door. She could handle this. She really could. "Okay, what can I bring?'' she asked, forcing herself to concentrate on practical matters.

Joe strode ahead to hold the door open for her. ''Just yourself.'' He waited for her to pass through ahead of him, then caught up with her in the hall.

''You're sure?'' Emma said, as they walked together side by side, their steps meshing perfectly.

''Positive,'' Joe reassured with a confident wink and a teasing grin. ''And come hungry, 'cause I'm a master outdoor barbecue chef.''

She tossed him a skeptical look and he said, ''Really.''

He pressed both hands to his chest modestly. ''I can tell by that look on your face you don't believe me, but it's true. Women have been known to *faint* when they eat a steak prepared by me,'' he teased.

Emma laughed. The man was incorrigible. ''Okay, okay, you've convinced me. I'll come hungry.''

''Good.''

She paused at her desk. She had a few more things to do before she could leave the office, though he was free to go on ahead of her. ''I'll see you around eight?'' Emma asked, feeling ridiculously happy—and not just because she'd just sold his house in record time.

Joe grinned back at her. ''Eight o'clock it is.''

''I SHOULD HAVE figured it would rain,'' Emma lamented to Joe as she approached the barbecue in his backyard. Not that the inclement weather seemed to have deterred Joe O'Reilly in any way. Smoke curled up in a charcoal plume and the coals were white as ash.

And as for Joe himself, he was more handsome than she had ever seen him in olive green shorts and a long, oversize white polo, worn open at the neck, shirttails out.

Emma cast an unhappy look at the sky, where the gathering gray clouds looked ready to rain down on them at any second. "It happens every single time I plan a cookout."

"Shame on you," Joe said with a grin, "jinxing my cookout."

No sooner had he spoken than raindrops pelted them in the face. Within seconds they were falling harder. Emma stepped back beneath the edges of the roof, watching with disappointment as the rain began. "If you want to cancel, I'll understand."

"Hell, no." Joe slammed the lid on the grill and dashed up the back steps to the door. He ducked inside and returned with an umbrella, which he promptly opened, a platter of steak and a long-handled barbecue fork. "But if you want to wait for me inside—" he continued, not the least bit upset by the bad weather.

"Don't be silly," Emma said, happy to see he was so resilient. "If you can stand out here in the rain, so can I."

She took the umbrella and held it over both of them and the grill. Joe slid the steaks onto the rack. "Baked potatoes, too?" Emma asked, her mouth already watering as she looked down at the foil-wrapped packages already cooking in the coals.

"And corn on the cob, salad and some great Bordeaux," Joe confirmed. "When I go all out, I go all out."

"So where did you learn to cook like this?" Emma said, long minutes later, as they sat on the stoop beneath the overhang and ate with their plates on their knees. The rain continued steadily as darkness fell, enveloping them in a warm sensual mist.

"I taught myself mostly," Joe confided.

"How come?"

"Cause I got sick of Navy chow and it seemed stupid to ask a woman to do what I could do for myself."

Made sense. "Have there been many women in your life?" Emma asked before she could stop herself.

Joe looked at her in a way that let her know he was enjoying himself, then uttered a rueful laugh. "A few," he admitted nonchalantly. "No one who could hold a candle to you, though."

She took a deep shaky breath—they were heading into dangerous territory here—then sipped her wine. "I'm sorry. I shouldn't have asked that," she said.

Joe brushed aside her apology, letting her know it was unnecessary. "It's okay. I don't have any secrets from you, Emma." He paused. "I don't want to have any, either."

Neither do I, Joe.

"What we had back then was great and I have to admit sometimes I miss it, too, but realistically I know it's now that counts. Not the romantic—" he searched for a word and finally came up with "—love affair that we had then."

Emma missed what they'd had then, too. Nevertheless, she knew even if Joe didn't that it wasn't quite as simple and uncomplicated as he thought. Not with the lies she'd told him pooling like deadweight in her stomach. But she wouldn't think about that. Not tonight. "The potatoes are really good, too. What'd you do to them?"

"I nuked them in the microwave first, then put them on the grill." He kicked back, his elbows on the top step behind them, and tossed her a sexy grin. "Maybe I should write a cookbook. Make a million dollars."

Emma rolled her eyes. "Somehow I can't picture you in an apron, demonstrating recipes on a television show," she told him dryly.

He sighed. "Guess not."

Emma looked down at her nearly empty plate. She was stuffed. A glance at the wine bottle between them showed a third of a bottle left. Joe's glass was empty. "Want to finish off the Bordeaux?" she asked.

"I'll probably need it to tackle the kitchen," Joe said. "It's one hell of a mess."

Emma grinned and stretched her legs out parallel to his. The evening was so perfect, despite the rain, she almost hated to see it end. But she didn't have to go, yet. "I'll help you clean up," she promised.

"Naw, you're my guest."

"And your realtor, but I can still wash a mean dish."

He sent her a look of silent thanks. "Okay," he said softly, "you're on."

Slowly, they picked up and moved into the house. Working in peaceful harmony, they finished the dishes and the rest of the wine, then curled up on the sofa together and started in on sinfully rich slices of a chocolate cake Joe had picked up at the corner bakery and cups of hot black coffee.

"That was the best meal I've had in a long time."

"Me, too. Although I think it was the company I liked, more than the cuisine—as excellent as it was," he added with a teasing, immodest grin.

"I'm glad the rain didn't spoil our cookout." She shook her head. "I was afraid when I saw the storm clouds that the whole evening would be off."

"On account of a little rain?" Joe stood and pulled her to her feet. Together, they carried their empty dishes to the kitchen and slid them into the hot soapy water in the sink. "No way."

She grinned at the determined look on his face, suddenly recalling how much fun it was just to be with Joe. "You haven't changed, have you?" she asked with reverent appreciation.

He leaned against the counter and gave her a quizzical look.

"When life throws you a lemon, you make lemonade."

Joe grinned and moved so that her back was to the counter and he was standing in front of her. "Yep," he agreed with her softly, "I do everything I can to make the most out of my life. And I also take advantage of the opportunities presented me."

That said, he took her face in his hands, his gaze lovingly skimming the blueness of her eyes, the tilt of her nose, the faintly pouty line of her lips, the stubborn line of her chin. "I missed you, Emma," he confessed in a ragged tone, all the love he felt in his heart evident on his face. "You'll never know how much."

And suddenly, there was no turning back, because Emma knew they were meant to be together. "I've missed you, too," she whispered emotionally. Hope and yearning flowing through her, she rose on tiptoe to meet his descending mouth and found his kiss every bit as hot and fiery and full of pent-up passion as she had imagined. Her arms laced around his broad back, and she savored the taste and smell and feel of him. He was so male, so deliciously hard and male and strong, she thought.

With a ragged breath, he tore his mouth from hers. Resting his forehead against hers, he closed his eyes. "Oh, God, Emma, I want you so much. I'm not going to be able to stop if we keep this up."

Emma had thought weeks ago that in many respects it seemed he had never left her, that in some intrinsic way she'd been tied to him from the beginning and was tied to him still. That feeling had multiplied a hundredfold. "I don't want you to stop, Joe," she confessed. She looked deep into his eyes, into his soul. And found only goodness. Only love. She released her breath in a trembling rush. "I want you to make love to me."

He looked at her long and hard, his conscience telling him he had no business even contemplating a move like this. But his heart was telling him to risk everything and go for broke. "Even when you know we've got no future?" He didn't want to say it, but he knew it had to be said.

Emma didn't have to be reminded that he was leaving again. But she also knew what he was trying to do in bringing it up. He was trying to save her—save them both—from being hurt. The trouble was they'd gone beyond that, way beyond. All they could do now was ease the pain of their eventual separation by making memories that would keep them both feeling both warm and loved for years to come. "Even then," she said quietly but firmly. Now was all that mattered. Joe was all that mattered. And right now she wanted to be with him more than she had ever wanted anything in her life.

Joe studied her, his yearning every bit as immediate as her own. To hell with his conscience, he thought, as he reached behind her wordlessly and locked the back door.

The next thing Emma knew she was being swept up into his arms and cradled against him as if she weighed no more than a feather. Joe strode back to the bedroom and nudged open the door with the toe of his shoe. It bounced as it hit the doorstop, the springy noise echoing in the silence of the house. Joe feigned annoyance at the sound and her barely contained laughter. "Now what?" Emma murmured.

Joe let her down slowly so the back of her knees were against the edge of the bed and the front of her was against the hard length of him. Emma didn't know it, she hadn't a clue, but it was all he could do not to take her now, hard and fast. But he couldn't do that to her. She deserved better.

Slowing his pulse deliberately, Joe let his gaze mesh with Emma's. Their eyes holding hypnotically, he teased, "What would you like to be next?" *That's it, take it nice and easy.*

The breath left Emma's lungs as she remembered without warning what a warm and indefatigably generous lover he could be. What did she want? She wanted everything, but most of all, she wanted him. "I want you to touch me," she said quietly.

Joe wanted that, too. More than Emma could ever know. She'd kept him up nights, dreaming of this, ever since he'd been back, ever since he'd felt her against him, length to length, that first night outside his house.

"Done." He slid his palms beneath the silky veil of her hair and cupped her head between his warm, hard hands. "But first this," he said, as he tilted her head back and delivered a kiss that was all consuming, all igniting in its demand.

They were trembling when they broke apart. Eyes still on hers, he tugged her T-shirt over her head. He traced his thumbs over the creamy flesh spilling out of the lacy cups of her bra, and slid the straps down to uncover the taut rosy peaks of her nipples. He brushed his thumbs over the hardening nubs, then bent and laved first one, and then the other with his tongue. Eyes closed, she let her head fall back as rivers of fire coursed through her and her insides fluttered with remembrance of all the pleasure he was capable of giving her.

Impatient to feel more of her, he unfastened her bra at the back and drew it down her arms. Shy, she moved her arms as if to cover herself. He held her arms apart from her body. "You don't ever have to be ashamed," he said softly, his eyes boring into hers. His glance lowered. He touched everywhere he looked. "You're so beautiful," he said, warmly covering her flesh with both palms, kneading her in slow, mesmerizing circles. "So soft, so satiny."

Emma felt beautiful. And impatient. She too wanted to taste, touch, feel. She pushed up the hem of his shirt, above the flat washboard stomach, above the hard male nipples and whorls of curling hair, and over the brawny width of his shoulders. It dropped to the floor beside her T-shirt. "I want to feel you against me," she whispered. She moved forward, standing on tiptoe, until their nipples touched and he groaned. Slowly, she lowered her heels to the floor again, dragging her upper body against his as she went. The friction of their bodies was delicious.

More restive now, he anchored her against him and kissed her fiercely, until there was no breath left in her body, until every inch of her was aching and throbbing and the muscles of his back were taut beneath the caressing ministrations of her open palms. She wanted him. Oh, how she wanted him. But she didn't want to rush. Not when they had waited so long.

He dropped kisses down the nape of her neck and across her collarbone as his hands worked with the front zipper of her shorts. He pushed them down, his thumb anchoring in the waistband of her bikini panties along the way. She kicked free of her shorts, the action momentarily spreading her legs. His thumb slid beneath the cloth, through the soft golden curls, to the rounded cleft. A current of white-hot sensation shimmered through her and she sighed his name, then sighed it once more as he touched her again. And then again.

"Off," she murmured, pushing at the thin waistband of her French-cut panties.

"No, not yet," he said, as he lowered her onto the bed, pulling her forward until her knees were at the edge of the mattress. Joe slid between them and left a trail of hot damp kisses over her skin, from shoulders to breasts, then dipped his tongue in her navel and continued his southward path. His lips were bliss, and agony. She wanted more, much more, but he made her wait. He caressed her slender thighs, his touch eliciting a million tiny tingles along her skin. Everywhere he touched, she burned. Unable to stay still, she shifted and moved with him until at last he joined her on the bed.

Her hands were already on the clasp of his shorts. He helped her get them off. His briefs followed just as swiftly. Confronted with the erect male sight of him, she was momentarily silent. And awed. Then she touched, and it was his turn to moan as she enveloped the satiny length of him with the softness of her palms and the stroking of her fingertips.

At last he could take no more. Taking her wrists in his hands, he guided them up until they rested against the mattress on either side of her head. Releasing her only long enough to divest her of her panties, he settled between her thighs. Their mouths met again, their tongues twining, mating. With her arms still trapped on either side of her, every inch of her melded against every inch of him, she felt deliciously, deliciously plundered.

"Now," he asked softly, between fervent kisses.

"Now," she confirmed with a wanton sigh.

She gasped as he entered, moaned as he moved inside her. Then she was moving, too, exquisite pleasure bolting through her with a shattering sensuality that left her weak. All this time...she hadn't known...hadn't realized it could be even better than before. She had never felt like this, so cherished and ravished and loved all at once. She had never wanted like this. "Joe," Emma murmured, as happiness catapulted inside her like an out-of-control sparkler on the Fourth of July, "oh, Joe..."

He released her hands and held her close. "Don't leave me again," she thought she heard him whisper. And then all was lost as they strained together, the storm outside nothing compared to the storm brewing between the two. *I'm in love with you, Joe,* Emma thought. *I always have been and I always will be...no matter what...*

Later, much later, Joe held her in his arms. The loneliness Emma had felt ever since he had left had vanished. In its place was sweet contentment. She refused to let herself think about the future, but Emma could tell, as the moment lengthened, that Joe was troubled both by what had just happened and what was to come.

"This isn't why I asked you over."

Emma cuddled closer and rested her head on the warm surface of his muscular chest, the soft ragged sounds of their breathing mingling with the comforting sounds of the steady summer rain outside. "I know, Joe." *You don't owe me an apology. I'm not a young girl anymore. You didn't take advantage.*

He sighed contentedly as he moved his fingers through her hair, admitting with a soft honest laugh, "Although I *have* wanted to make love to you for weeks now."

She grinned impishly and peered up at him through the veil of her lashes. "I know that, too." And she had enjoyed every erotic moment of their coming together.

"The problem is," Joe continued, looking suddenly troubled and reluctant, yet determined to hash this out now just the same, "I've only got another week . . ." And he wanted so much more time with Emma, he thought. So damned much more.

But Emma didn't want to think about the future, or the possible heartache ahead of them, or anything that might spoil the beauty of this night. She put a finger to his lips. "I know you're married to the Navy, Joe, I know you have duties and obligations. I just want to be with you this one last time."

Joe had thought that was what he wanted, too. One last time with her. "You're sure?" he asked huskily, knowing above all else he didn't want to hurt her. Unable to help himself he let his fingers rove tenderly over the planes of her face. "You won't hate me when this is all over and I have to leave again?"

Emma sighed. "We're not kids anymore, Joe," she admitted wearily. "I knew going into this that we had separate lives, careers, adult responsibilities. There's no way for us to be together long term." For so many reasons, the secrets she still held in her heart not the least of them. "But that doesn't have to matter now, does it?"

He flashed her an ironic grin. "Funny that you should be saying these things to me," he said, his eyes sad but accepting. "In the past those would've been my lines."

She took his hand and pressed it to her lips. "I've learned to take what I can get out of life and be grateful for that much." *I no longer reach for what I can't have.*

Generally, Joe did, too.

"It'll be enough," she continued to soothe, drinking in the salty taste of his skin as Joe reached for her again. It would be enough because it would have to be....

Chapter Twelve

"Well, it's over. You've closed on the house," Emma said to Joe. "The Kosteleckys take possession Monday."

"And I leave on Sunday."

Both were silent as they walked from the attorney's office to her car. Emma slid in behind the wheel. Her fingers numb with tension, she started the car and backed out of the lot. *I can't believe it's over this quickly,* she thought as she guided her car expertly onto the busy suburban street. They had been lovers again for one week. It seemed like forever and yet not nearly long enough. "Do you want me to drop you at home?" she said, forcing normalcy into her tone.

This was going to be okay. She had known, going in, that Joe was leaving again. She'd told herself she could handle their inevitable breakup, that all she had needed was this one short week. Now she knew how wrong she had been. Not that it mattered. The fact that her heart was breaking into thousands of tiny pieces didn't change a thing.

"It depends. What are you going to do?" Joe asked.

Emma tightened her hands on the steering wheel. She was determined not to act like a lovesick idiot about this. "I thought I'd go back to the office," she said calmly, although she was furiously fighting a film of tears that made it increasingly difficult for her to see. "I need to clear up some paperwork there." *Anything to get my mind off you, Joe.*

Joe looked at her long and hard, seeing in an instant everything she was working so hard to hide. "Pull over," he commanded gruffly. When she didn't respond fast enough, he growled it again. "Pull over, I said."

Her heart in her throat, Emma did as he asked, sliding her car neatly into a space in front of the bank. Joe got out and circled around to the driver's side. "I'm driving."

Emma knew from the grim set of his mouth there was no arguing with him. She unfastened her seat belt and slid over into the passenger seat. So much for not acting like an idiot, she thought. Nevertheless, she felt compelled to point out dryly, "It's my car."

"You don't have to tell me that," he said as he folded his tall body behind the wheel and then adjusted the seat to the farthest position out.

"Then why...?"

Joe checked over his shoulder, saw a hole in the traffic and pulled out. "You can't drive when you're crying." He fastened his seat belt while he drove.

"I wasn't—"

"Yes, Emma," he interrupted in an unbearably weary, beleaguered tone, "you were."

She sniffed and looked out the window, irritated he'd seen fit to point out her shortcomings when she'd been doing her level best to ignore his. "So I get emotional at closings."

Joe sent her a concerned look, whatever he was feeling very well concealed. "Is that all it was?"

She breathed in deeply through her nose. In, out. In, out. "You're lacking tact here, Joe." That said, she stared straight ahead.

"I know," he said, turning down their street. "It happens to me sometimes. But, lady, you haven't seen anything yet." He pulled into his driveway with a screech, then darted out of the car, around to her side. Too piqued to be the least bit of help, Emma sat where she was, seat belt on. She didn't appreciate being treated like a dim child. "Now what?" she asked as he pulled open the passenger door on her side with the same annoying enthusiasm.

Joe grinned. "Tell you what," he said, leaning over to unfasten her shoulder harness, his hand brushing her breasts as he did. "I'll surprise you." The next thing Emma knew he had her by the hand and was guiding her from the car. She didn't stay on her feet long, however. The moment she was up and out of the car, he took her into his arms. Very aware that it was broad daylight and there was more than one neighbor out cutting the lawn or checking their mail, Emma said, "What do you think you're doing?" The skirt of her business suit was hiked halfway up her thighs.

Joe was already striding implacably toward the house. "What I should have done years ago," he said. "If you want me to do it *in* the house, reach in my pocket and get my keys."

"Joe—"

He shrugged and pretended to set her down on the front porch. "Okay with me if we do it out here."

Deciding from the amorous glint in his eyes that probably wasn't a good idea, Emma said, "No. Wait."

He grinned at her knowingly and demanded, "The keys."

Flushed, Emma used the arm that was not looped around his neck to fish in his pockets for his house key. She found it all right, and a whole lot more. "You're not being very mysterious," she teased, with a mischievous glance below his belt.

"That's what you think." He nodded his head in the direction of the door, then threatened, "Give it a try, Emma, or I swear I'll do what I have in mind right here, right now."

Emma had only to look deep into those golden brown eyes of his to know he damn well meant what he said. With fingers that shook she slid the key in the door. "This would be a whole lot simpler if you just put me down," she said.

The lock clicked. Impatient as ever, Joe shoved open the door with his foot. "Emma, there are some things you're in charge of," he replied, mocking her dry tone to a T. *"Not this."*

Once inside, he shut the door with his foot. "Thank heavens for small miracles," Emma sighed.

He lifted a quizzical brow in her direction.

"I think," she said wryly, "the neighbors have already seen quite enough for one day, thank you very much."

Joe chuckled softly, the low sexy sound of his voice echoing through the silence of the rooms, and kept going. *Well, this is a new one,* Emma thought, looping both her arms about his strong neck. She still felt like crying, but she was diverted now, too, her heart already thudding a heavy, anticipatory beat. "I've never been carried off caveman-style before."

"My mistake," he said.

Joe wasn't even the tiniest bit out of breath as he lowered her very, very gently to the bed. She lay back against the pillows, curious as to what he was going to do next. Then she decided she was making everything far too easy and rose up again, on her elbows. He leaned forward to slip off her heels, tossed them aside, got rid of his own shoes and sat down beside her. "So far so good. Now what?" Emma said.

"I don't know." Joe pretended to be perplexed, to comic effect. "Isn't this where the Tooth Fairy comes in? Or do I have the wrong story?"

"You've got the wrong story." She paused. "I think."

"I don't think so," he said gently, pushing back a lock of her golden hair and tucking it behind her ear. He bent forward and pressed a kiss to her temple very very gently. "Why don't you give it a try? Look under your pillow, Emma."

Emma stared at him. Her heart pounding harder than ever, she sat all the way up, pulled the bedspread back, and lifted the pillow. Beneath it was a velvet box. Not the small kind, which contained rings, but the wide rectangular kind that generally held necklaces. Emma swallowed hard. He'd really had her going there. Fool that she was, she'd thought—hoped—he was going to ask her to marry him. But he hadn't done so before, and he certainly wasn't going to take that step now. Probably this was some type of token, a payment for one red-hot week.

Humiliation filled her cheeks. She knew her face must be scarlet.

"Go on. Open it," he urged gently, still watching her face.

Emma did. Inside was what she had expected—a beautiful gold rope necklace, bracelet and earrings to match.

"That," Joe said softly as he lifted her hand and kissed her open palm, "is for listing and selling my house and all the thousand and one things you did before and after to ensure everything ran smoothly."

Emma forced back the lump in her throat. "I was glad to help." *Just let me get through this,* she wished fervently, with some self-respect still intact.

"And this," Joe said softly, reaching beneath his pillow and pulling out a much, much smaller velvet box from the very same jewelers. "Is from me. Because you're you."

Emma stared at it, tears gathering in her eyes. She wanted an engagement ring so very much that she was afraid to open the box. Afraid she would be disappointed and that it would show and Joe would find out she wasn't the fiercely independent career woman who would never ever marry again that she'd told him she was. "You didn't have to do all this," Emma said, delaying the moment of truth. She didn't want to be left again. She didn't want them to part at all. She didn't think she could bear it.

"Too late—I think I already did." Joe was continuing to watch her, a guarded expression on his face.

Emma wished he would kiss her, reassure her. But suddenly he looked as tense and nervous and uncertain as she felt. Knowing there was no other option, she decided to end the suspense and open the box. Inside was a diamond surrounded by six diamond chips. "Do you like it?" Joe asked.

"It's beautiful," Emma said, but she still didn't know quite what it meant.

He shook his head in obvious regret, looking troubled by the way things had worked out. "I wish we'd had more time," he said, taking a deep breath.

That was what this was, then? A goodbye gift? A "thanks, I'll be seeing you around" gift? The tears she'd been withholding for what seemed an eternity now welled up and spilled heedlessly out over her lashes. Emma had never felt more foolish. "So do I," she said thickly as she dashed the tears away and tried to quell the depth of her disappointment.

He took the ring from the box and slipped it onto the ring finger of her left hand. It was a half size or so too big and they both stared at it in silence. In all the years she had known him, Joe O'Reilly had never been at a loss for words. He'd been too angry to speak to her occasionally, but never had he not known what to say. Until today.

Finally, he shook his head in derision. "I'm doing this all wrong." Abruptly, he got up from the bed and, shoving his hands in the back pockets of his pants, began to pace the small bedroom. "I had it all planned out. I knew just what I was going to say and do—"

He paused, his eyes roving her face. In that instant Emma saw past his good intentions and his clumsiness and knew he had never loved her more than he did at that instant. The next thing she knew he was back down on the bed beside her, taking her into his arms and holding her close. The fear that it was both too soon and too late faded away. It didn't matter what the ring meant, she told herself firmly, he still cared about her. He didn't want to say goodbye!

"Damn it, Emma, yes or no," he demanded hoarsely in a voice that told her his patience was exhausted. *"Will you marry me or not?"*

She drew back so she could see his face. "Marry you?" she echoed in disbelief, not sure she had actually heard the words she had so longed for him to say.

"I know, I know." He held up a hand in stop-signal fashion, not giving her a chance to speak. "It's all happening damn fast and even if you do, it'll be a hell of a life. You'll have to give up your job here—or maybe you won't, I don't know, I guess you could stay here if you wanted to and make it your and Bobby's permanent base—while I move around from place to place. You'll have to endure my long absences and adjust to the rigors of being a Navy wife, but I really think given time and a lot of effort on both our—"

"Yes," Emma said simply.

Joe stared at her. "Yes?"

"Yes." She laughed happily, feeling weak with the depth of her relief, that it wasn't over yet between her and Joe and, God willing, would never be. "And—I thought you'd never ask."

Joe's lips twisted wryly. "You told me you never wanted to get married again," he reminded her with exaggerated sternness.

"I didn't want to get married again," Emma said, sighing. She let herself look into his eyes until every bit of fear was gone and all she felt was the love flowing between them. "Not until I fell in love with you all over again," she finished softly. The next thing she knew she was in Joe's arms. He was kissing her long and hard and holding her tight enough to crack ribs. "I love you, too," he whispered fiercely in her ear.

"I know." Emma basked in the tenderness of his embrace. They kissed again, leisurely this time, then drew apart slowly, both of them knowing they had all the time in the world.

Abruptly, Joe's look became troubled once again. "What about Bobby?" He paused. "How do you think he'll take all this?"

Emma was not worried about her son. "It'll be fine. Bobby adores you, Joe."

"Sure, as a friend of the family and neighbor. As a stepdad, I don't know."

At the oblique reference to Bobby's paternity, guilt stabbed Emma like a knife, reminding her sharply of all she strove so hard to forget. Suddenly, she had to get up. Oh, God, she finally had everything she had always wanted and her life was falling apart. Because she knew now what she had refused to face, that she couldn't be with Joe, not on any permanent basis, with the lie about Bobby standing between them. *She had to tell him.* But first, she had to tell Skip.

Determined to hide the extent of her misery from Joe, she looked around for her shoes. "I have to talk to Skip," she said. "Tell him we're getting married." And the rest.

Joe didn't argue about the necessity of such a task, merely offered promptly, "Okay, I'll go with you."

One shoe on, Emma whirled toward him. Envisioning how Skip would react if he heard the news about their impending marriage from Joe, she said, "No!" Her voice was sharp, too sharp. Joe started and she forced herself to calm down and take it easy. "No, I have to talk to him, Joe, alone."

She had to make Skip understand that they could no longer go on with the lies and the deceptions, not if she was going to marry Joe. As difficult as it was, Joe had to be told the truth. Only if he knew what she'd done and forgave her could she marry him.

Joe's gaze narrowed. He wasn't pleased with her decision to go it alone. "Skip may not take this well," he warned. "In fact, judging from his behavior at Bobby's graduation, we have every reason to believe he won't."

Emma knew that. She also knew she had no choice but to reach him, to make him see things her way. In the end, she had the feeling she would need Skip's help with Joe. "Skip is a good man," she countered firmly. Emma found her other shoe and slipped her foot into it. "A caring, decent man. I have every confidence in the end he will do the right thing." *Just as I am now,* she thought.

Joe looked confused. "You mean give us his blessing?"

Emma nodded curtly. She knew from the look on Joe's face that he was confused. "His blessing and his promise to help us work this out with Bobby, of course," Emma said. "I just think," she finished gently, "that he'll take it better if I tell him—alone—first."

Joe's shoulders relaxed slightly. "I see what you mean," he said finally. The look in his golden brown eyes grew distant. "Maybe that would be better," he said quietly.

Emma glanced at her watch. "Their plane was supposed to land an hour ago. Skip told me he was going to take Bobby straight back to his place—"

"You're going over there now?" Joe's expression was incredulous.

She pushed his disbelief away. She knew he wanted to make love to her, to celebrate her saying yes, but there was no time for that now. Not when there was so very much at stake. "Yes," she said. "I am. I've got to."

Chapter Thirteen

Joe sat in his bedroom long after Emma had driven away. She was wearing the engagement ring, but the necklace, bracelet and earrings were in their velvet box.

He still couldn't believe she'd walked out on him that way. He could sympathize with her wanting to get everything worked out as swiftly as possible, of course. He wanted the same thing. But what he couldn't understand was the nervous, haunting look on her face as she left. He had the feeling she was keeping secrets again. And a marriage based on secrets was no damn good at all.

Maybe it was his imagination. Maybe she and Skip didn't have any secrets. Maybe it was just the last of the old guilt, coupled with her wanting to protect Bobby.

He pictured Skip's getting the news from Emma. He thought of the two of them in the cafeteria after Bobby's graduation, recalled the stressed look on Emma's face, and knew he'd made a mistake letting her go off alone. She might be a grown woman, mature and independent, but there were some things she shouldn't have to handle alone, and this was one of them. Besides, Skip would probably take it better if he knew Joe had no intention of trying to usurp Skip's position in Bobby's life. He loved Bobby. He could easily imagine being a father to him. But he didn't want to ruin the solid, stable family life Bobby already had, especially since Bobby had already weathered the hardship of a divorce.

EMMA'S CAR was in front of Skip's house. The windows were open. Eager to be with her, Joe moved swiftly and soundlessly up the walk. And that was when he heard Skip's voice, his tone vehement, through the open living room windows.

"Emma, we can't tell Joe the truth now, after all these years!"

"Joe has a right to know, Skip!" Emma's voice was low and stressed and tense.

Right to know what? Joe wondered. But he had no chance to figure it out because Skip was already going on, demanding tersely, "What about Bobby?"

Defensively, Emma replied, "We don't have to tell Bobby, not yet."

Skip laughed harshly. "You really think Joe's going to keep it a secret?"

Keep what a secret? Joe thought, his aggravation growing.

"I—"

"He has a son, Emma," Skip intervened, cutting her off. "A son he never knew about. All these years—"

A son . . . ? He had a son?

"All these years, we've kept Bobby away from him. How the hell is he going to forgive you for that?"

Joe had the impression he was in shock, then everything blurred. The next thing he knew he was standing in the open doorway of Skip's home, staring into the ashen faces of Emma and Skip. The woman he loved and his ex-best friend. He'd never felt angrier or more betrayed in his life. And Emma, damn her lying soul to hell, had never been more desperate.

"Joe," she said, stricken, sobbing, "we can explain—"

In that instant, as he looked from Emma's face to Skip's, Joe knew what it was like to want to kill with his bare hands. "I'll bet you can," he said grimly.

Emma swallowed. "We wanted to tell you."

"Sure." Joe heard his own voice, icy and calm. Too calm.

"But I couldn't—" Emma continued tearfully.

Joe thought about all the lost years with his son, and with Emma. He could have had a family! But Emma had robbed him of that. Robbed him of everything. And then, damn her, she had the audacity to stand there and pretend that none of this was her fault? She couldn't tell him? "Why the hell not?" he growled.

A terrified look on her face, Emma clasped her hands together in front of her. "Because if you'd known I was pregnant you would've stayed here and married me," she whispered miserably, the tears still streaming wetly down her face.

It was all Joe could do not to shake her within an inch of her life. But he had never touched a woman in anger and he wasn't about to start. "Damn right about that much," he snarled.

Emma's lower lip trembled and she turned her bright blue eyes on him, silently beseeching him to understand as she whispered sadly, "Yes, Joe, you would have stayed here and done your duty to me and to your son." Her voice dropped another accusing notch. "And then you would've hated me the rest of your life." She came forward, pleading, "I knew how much you wanted to go to the academy. And I knew that if I told you, or if the academy found out you had a dependent, you would have automatically been denied your appointment. It wouldn't have mattered whether you married me or not. Just the fact you had a child would've been enough to get you dismissed."

What she was saying made sense. Vaguely. But she had also robbed him of choice. And that he couldn't forgive her for. "So you married my best friend instead!" Joe thundered.

Skip stepped forward in Emma's defense. "She was going to run away. Have the baby alone in a big city. I couldn't let her do that. Not with your child."

"Yeah, some friend you were," Joe said bitterly, unable to believe Skip was acting as if he had done Joe some big noble favor by stealing his girl. "You couldn't wait to hop into her bed."

Skip looked as weary as Emma. "It wasn't like that. She didn't even tell me she was pregnant. I guessed, when I saw her being sick." Skip's voice was calm, logical.

But Joe had already heard enough. He was turning, heading out of the house for his car. Emma raced after him. "Joe! What are you going to do?"

Unable to bear her touch, to bear anything about her, he shrugged her off. "I don't know."

And still, she wouldn't let him go, still she felt compelled to explain. "I never planned to stay married to Skip, Joe, at least not in the beginning. Our relationship was completely platonic until well after the first year, until after Bobby was born."

Joe could believe that but it didn't make any difference. His body rigid with suppressed rage and pain, he whirled on Emma. "Is that supposed to make me feel better, the fact that you waited to crawl into bed with him? Am I supposed to award you some medal of honor for that?"

She drew herself up to her full five-foot-six height. "I'm trying to tell you how it was." Anger flashed in her bright blue eyes. "Are you going to listen, or not?"

Joe didn't want to, but he also knew Emma, and if she was determined he know everything, he would end up hearing it sooner or later, anyway. His jaw feeling as if it had been carved in marble, he waited impatiently for her to go on.

Emma took a ragged breath and went on in a calmer tone of voice. "After Bobby was born, everything changed. We both loved him so much, from the very beginning, and we knew he deserved a loving, stable home. I began to see I couldn't possibly rear him alone, not when he was that little. Skip wanted to be there for both of us, so we decided to try to make our marriage a real one." She shook her head, her pain every bit as real as his own, then went on in a tortured whisper, "We thought we could make it work, but it never did. I was still in love with you, and always have been."

Her kind of love Joe didn't need.

Emma rushed on. "I didn't want to hurt you, Joe. But what choice did I have? Tell you I was pregnant and rob you of your lifelong dream to attend the academy? Go somewhere else and have the baby on welfare? Or marry Skip and give my child both a father and a name?"

For her the solution was obvious. For Joe it was not. "The baby had a father!" And he still could have had a career in the Navy without going to the academy!

Emma's eyes flashed a warning. "I begged you to stay here, Joe, to go to college here on an ROTC scholarship, but you wouldn't even discuss the possibility!" She threw up her slender arms angrily. "So what was I supposed to do? Have you marry me for the baby's sake and hate me and the child for the rest of your life?"

Emma wasn't the only one fighting tears. "I would never have hated Bobby," Joe said.

Emma shook her head in silent disagreement. "It's so easy for you to say that now, when you've already lived all your dreams," she told him wearily, then focused the brunt of her ravaged expression on him. "You forget, I've seen the flip side of that coin," she reminded him bitterly. "I saw what giving up his dreams to rear a child did to my father. It made him impossible, frustrated and resentful. I wasn't about to do the same thing to you. Being the yoke around someone's neck once was more than enough. I had lived that way for years, I wasn't about to do it again!''

But all Joe could think about was the lies they'd told, and what he'd lost because of them. Emma had robbed him of his son for eleven whole years. He had missed the entire first decade of his son's life and that was something he could never get back.

Suddenly, he'd heard all the excuses and the rationalization he could take. It was time they got down to the truth, as hard to swallow as it might be. "Answer me this," he demanded roughly, searching Emma's upturned face. "If I hadn't come back, if we hadn't picked up our affair again, would you ever have told me the truth?"

Emma said nothing, but the answer was as clear as the pain in her eyes.

JOE RATTLED AROUND his empty house. Dawn was breaking, and he was exhausted and no closer to a solution than he had been the night before. At first he'd been too damn angry to think clearly, but now so much was coming back to him.

Emma, crying her eyes out the day he left for the academy. Emma, trying every way possible—save telling him the sobering truth—to get him to change his mind and give up the appointment to the academy. Not because he was being forced to do so, but because he loved her.

Fool that he was, he had never suspected for a minute anything else was wrong. Skip had seen the early
signs of her pregnancy, but not Joe. No, he'd been so
full of himself in those days, so caught up in his own
dreams, so sure she would wait for him that he'd gone
off blithely thinking everything would work out in the
end, that Emma would wait for him, they'd see each
other during vacations, talk on the phone, write and
get married after he graduated.

So Emma, afraid and alone, had made the only
choice she could. She had reached out to Skip the
same way a drowning person reaches for a lifesaver
ring.

Once the die was cast, there had been no turning
back. Skip's name was on Bobby's birth certificate
along with Emma's. The two were married. They had
made a home together. He was still at the academy and
had vowed never to speak to either of them.

And again, they had done the only thing they could.
They had carried on the best they knew how.

How could he fault her for that?

How could he fault Skip?

How could he blame either of them, especially when
he knew they all had been just kids?

EMMA WATCHED the sun come up slowly in the sky.
Joe was leaving today. Going back to Washington. His
house was sold. In all probability she would never see
him again, unless...oh, God, he wouldn't tell Bobby,
would he? He wouldn't try to claim his son, now, after all these years?

She sat down weakly, glad Bobby was over at Skip's house. It would have been too much for her to have to pretend everything was fine this morning when her whole world was falling apart.

Yesterday, she had been the happiest she had ever been in her life. Joe had told her he loved her and asked her to marry him. And she had been naively confident enough in that love of his to want to risk telling him the truth about Bobby. If only she'd been given the chance... If only he hadn't followed her to Skip's and overheard...

Maybe it would have all been different. And maybe it wouldn't have, she thought tiredly. Joe had never been one to pull his punches. He wanted a woman who was loyal and steadfast, a woman he could trust. How could he trust her now?

Emma stared out the window, at their twin back-yards, her cup of coffee in hand. Joe's house was as silent as her own. She wanted so very badly to talk to him one last time, but he was probably still asleep.

THEY MET HALFWAY between the two yards.

Emma had been geared to tell him one more time how much she loved him, but now as she looked at him, so rugged and handsome and indomitable, she didn't know where to begin. Joe did.

"Your place or mine?" he said simply.

"How about your back steps," Emma said. It seemed fitting somehow that their goodbye, if that's what it was going to be, take place there, since that was where they had met again.

Joe opened the back gate, followed her to the stoop and sat down beside her. The June morning was warm and humid, but Emma didn't care; she was just so glad to have this one last chance to be with him.

"Where's Bobby?" Joe asked with quiet protectiveness.

Emma's heart began a rapid beat. To still the trembling of her hands, she wrapped her arms about her upraised knees. "Still at Skip's," she said.

Joe nodded, his features relaxing ever so slightly. The silence went on. Emma tightened her clasped arms about her legs and tried to read what he was thinking, but she was unable to do so. Like any mother fiercely protecting her offspring, she wanted to order Joe not to hurt Bobby, to not tell him anything. But so many choices regarding Bobby's upbringing had already been denied Joe.

Unable to completely suppress her unease, she asked quietly, "What are you going to do?" Maybe it was time she let him make all the choices, she decided, even knowing how very hard it was going to be for her to do.

Joe took a deep breath and looked out at the rose-bushes the two of them had uncovered and brought back to life. They weren't blooming yet, but Emma knew they would.

"I want to tell him," Joe said, and at his decision, Emma's heart plummeted in her chest. She had been so hopeful that Joe would see things her way and want only to shield Bobby from the misery they all felt.

Oblivious to her thoughts, Joe swallowed hard and went on. "I want him to know he's my son and I love him. I want him to know that I loved him even before I knew he was my son." Joe ran a hand through his hair and released a ragged breath. "But I can't, Emma." He turned to her, beseeching her to understand. "This isn't something Bobby or any kid should be expected to handle. Not now. And maybe, just maybe, not ever."

Happy they were in agreement about this, after all, Emma blew out a relieved breath.

His eyes searched hers gently, his anger gone. "But that doesn't mean I have to turn my back on him," he continued quietly, after a moment, the affection he felt for his son clear. "I want to continue to be a part of his life," Joe said firmly. "From here on out, no matter what."

Emma tensed. Joe was being wonderful, as far as Bobby went, but as for the rest of what he was saying, it all sounded suspiciously like a carefully thought out prelude to a goodbye speech. "As a family friend?" she asked. Her spirits sank when he nodded.

"And *his* friend," he said simply.

So this was it. I should have expected this, but fool that I was, I didn't. Her throat clogged with tears, Emma studied the dew shining wetly on the grass.

"But Bobby isn't the reason I was coming over to talk to you," Joe said. He pried her arms from her legs and directed her to face him. When she had, he went on softly. "I came to talk to you about us, Emma." His golden brown eyes searched hers and he sighed. "I said some ugly things yesterday. I don't know if you can forgive me . . ." he began uncertainly.

Was he offering her simple friendship again? She only knew for certain that she wanted much more than that. "You had every right to be hurt and angry," she rushed to reassure him. Shaking her head ruefully, she continued, "I realize now I should have told you all along. But I didn't...because I was afraid." Tears clogged her voice. "I robbed you of the right to choose, Joe," she said, looking deep into his eyes. "I robbed you of your son." She released a sigh of abject misery, confessing, "And I am so sorry for that. I was trying to protect you, but instead I made everything so much worse."

Joe tightened both his hands on hers. "You and Skip were just kids then, Emma. We all were. You did the best you could under the circumstances, and that's all anyone can ever ask. Besides, I'm at fault here, too. If I hadn't been so caught up in my future career, I would've realized something was wrong. But I didn't because I didn't want to know. I left you, arrogantly sure we could work everything out, that you would wait for me. It was because of my attitude, my self-centeredness when it came to achieving my goals, that you felt you couldn't tell me."

"Does this mean you forgive me?" Emma asked in a voice husky with emotion.

Joe nodded. "With all my heart and soul," he whispered, then stood and drew her into his arms. "Can you forgive me?"

Emma nodded and looped her arms around his neck. She had made mistakes. They both had. But she knew now there was nothing they couldn't work out if they tried. And she would never, ever be afraid to go to him with the truth again. "There's nothing to forgive." She embraced him tightly. "Oh, Joe, I love you so much."

"I love you, too." His words were soft and warm against her ear. Drawing back slightly, he made his way to her mouth, and once there, kissed her long and hard and deep. "And I still want you to marry me," he murmured the minute they both came up for air. His golden eyes were somber, penitent and full of love as he finished with a gently teasing smile, "If you'll have me, that is."

"If?" Emma repeated, laughing through her tears. Unable to resist joshing him back, she pressed an index finger against her chin and struck an exaggeratedly thoughtful pose. "Gee, I'll have to think about it," she teased.

He grinned and gave her a squeeze.

Emma stopped laughing and kissed him full on the lips. "The answer is yes, Joe," she whispered, "yes!"

Epilogue

"Happy anniversary!" Joe whispered. "Can you believe we've been married almost three years now?"

"It seems like just yesterday that we got married," Emma murmured. And since then, it was hard for Emma to believe how well everything had gone. Three and a half years had passed since Joe had learned the truth. The first six months had been difficult, but after a lot of long heart-to-heart talks, he and Skip had repaired their friendship.

United in their concern about Bobby, both had made some sacrifices. Joe had promised to keep his career in the Washington, D.C. area until Bobby went off to college, and to do so, had taken a semipermanent job as an instructor at the academy. Skip had taken a job teaching economics at Georgetown University. Their split custody arrangement had continued—and would until Bobby left for college. Since both men had proved enormously supportive of each other, Emma had every reason to believe it would continue to work out. None of it had been easy, she reflected with a satisfied smile, but then, nothing worthwhile ever was.

"Hey, I heard you sold a mansion," Skip said.

Emma nodded. She had joined a Washington, D.C., firm and was still selling real estate. "One of the perks of doing business in this town is that whenever the administration changes, so do a lot of jobs. There's never any down time in the housing market, or so it seems." Knowing Skip had come to the party with the same beautiful woman he'd been squiring about town for the past nine months, Emma murmured, "It looks like you and Regina are getting serious."

Skip smiled shyly. "How does another June wedding sound to you?"

Emma hugged him, "Wonderful." Joe shook his hand.

Empty plate in hand, Bobby strolled over to join the group. "When are you going to cut the cake?" he asked impatiently, as if he were literally starving, although Emma had just seen him devour, not one, not two, but three plates of the buffet table food. At fifteen, he had grown tall and lanky. He'd traded his glasses for contacts and now spent equal time with both his computer and sports.

"Hungry again?" Joe asked, laughing.

Bobby made a guilty-as-charged face and patted his increasingly muscled stomach. "The original bottomless pit," he explained.

"Never a truer word was spoken," Skip agreed.

Bobby went to get his camera, Skip went to claim his new love and Joe and Emma headed for the table where the three-tiered cake was set up. All was in gleaming readiness. Joe looked around with a frown. "I think the knife's in the kitchen," Joe said.

"No, it's not—" Emma started to say as he pulled her behind the swinging doors of the reception hall kitchen and into a cozy corner.

Joe took her into his arms. "I know where the knife is. I just wanted a moment alone with my gorgeous wife," he said, pressing light, adoring kisses to her brow. "And you are just that. Gorgeous and sweet and loving and sexy and smart." Each compliment was punctuated with a kiss that made Emma glow.

"Keep going," Emma grinned, liking the warmth she felt all over.

Joe smiled back, eyed her up and down and delivered another long, lingering kiss to her temple. "Modest, too," he murmured, then kissed her again, and again.

At last they drew apart slowly and regarded each other in happy silence. Still gazing at her with mesmerizing intensity, Joe cleared his throat. "So where were we?" he asked, looking as if he had the vague idea they were supposed to be doing something but was all too willing to be distracted again.

Emma knew how he felt; she was equally dazzled by him. "We're supposed to be looking for the knife that's out there on the cake table," she reminded dryly.

"Oh, yeah. Well, what's a little diversion, especially when it brings me a few moments alone with my wonderful wife."

"Good point." Emma laced her arms about his neck, feeling the deep and lasting contentment that was so much a part of her life these days. "And as for time alone with me, that you can have any day," she promised, standing on tiptoe to kiss his lips, "and every day."

Joe tightened his arms around her waist and kissed her back. At that moment, Emma knew she'd never been happier in her life.

HE HAD TO BE REAL

Did ghosts have silky hair and piercing eyes? Were their bodies lean and hard? Emily Morrell didn't think so. But Captain Calvert T. Witherspoon, late of His Majesty's service, *was* walking through walls. Emily heard the rumors about Henderson House being haunted, but she didn't know her intoxicating fantasy ghost was more man than she could handle.

CHARLOTTE MACLAY brings you a delightful tale next month, about a ghost with a very special touch . . .

#488 A GHOSTLY AFFAIR
by Charlotte Maclay
May 1993

When a man loves a woman, there's nothing he wouldn't do for her. . . .

For a close encounter of the most sensual kind, don't miss American Romance #488 A GHOSTLY AFFAIR.

HG